Welcome to…

The Hollywood Hills Clinic

*Where doctors to the stars work miracles by day—
and explore their hearts' desires by night!*

When hotshot doc James Rothsberg started the clinic
six years ago he dreamed of a world-class facility,
catering to Hollywood's biggest celebrities,
and his team are unrivalled in their fields.
Now, as the glare of the media spotlight grows, the
Hollywood Hills Clinic is teaming up with the pro-bono
Bright Hope Clinic, and James is reunited with
Dr Mila Brightman…the woman he jilted at the altar!

When it comes to juggling the care of Hollywood A-listers
with care for the underprivileged kids of LA *anything* can
happen…and sizzling passions run high in the shadow of
the red carpet. With everything at stake for James,
Mila and the Hollywood Hills Clinic medical team
their biggest challenges have only just begun!

The Hollywood Hills Clinic miniseries:

Dear Reader,

Have you ever done something to protect a loved one? Something that hurt so deeply you thought you might never recover, but you did it anyway? Not everyone has had to make sacrifices like that, but I think most of us are willing to if it means the security and happiness of that other person.

This is the position that James Rothsberg found himself in when he unexpectedly fell for Mila Brightman. Only once he dropped the axe on their relationship he never expected to see her again. Years later Mila is back in town, and the two are forced to work together for the benefit of their community. And in doing so they find old feelings resurfacing at the worst of times.

Thank you for joining James and Mila as they struggle to get past old hurts and uncover secrets they thought long buried. And maybe—just maybe—they'll rediscover love along the way. I hope you enjoy reading their story as much as I loved writing it! Enjoy!

Love,

Tina Beckett

WINNING BACK HIS DOCTOR BRIDE

BY
TINA BECKETT

MILLS & BOON

First published in Great Britain 2016
By Mills & Boon, an imprint of HarperCollins*Publishers*
1 London Bridge Street, London, SE1 9GF

Large Print edition 2017

© 2016 Harlequin Books S.A.

Special thanks and acknowledgement are given to Tina Beckett for her contribution to The Hollywood Hills Clinic *series.*

ISBN: 978-0-263-06672-2

Three-time Golden Heart® finalist **Tina Beckett** learned to pack her suitcases almost before she learned to read. Born to a military family, she has lived in the United States, Puerto Rico, Portugal and Brazil. In addition to travelling, Tina loves to cuddle with her pug, Alex, spend time with her family, and hit the trails on her horse. Learn more about Tina from her website, or 'friend' her on Facebook.

Books by Tina Beckett

Mills & Boon Medical Romance

Midwives On-Call at Christmas
Playboy Doc's Mistletoe Kiss

New York City Docs
Hot Doc from Her Past

Midwives On-Call
Her Playboy's Secret

One Night That Changed Everything
NYC Angels: Flirting with Danger
The Lone Wolf's Craving
Her Hard to Resist Husband
The Dangers of Dating Dr Carvalho
To Play With Fire
His Girl From Nowhere
How to Find a Man in Five Dates
The Soldier She Could Never Forget

Visit the Author Profile page
at millsandboon.co.uk for more titles.

To my husband and children…always!

PROLOGUE

Six years ago

THERE WERE CERTAIN benefits to returning to civilization, texting being one of them.

Without it, she doubted she would survive this party.

No. Not party. "Charity event," as these A-listers liked to call their swanky affairs.

Whatever.

Mila Brightman's thumbs glided over the keys with remembered ease.

I will let u know.

C'mon, Mila. He's gorgeous and newly single.

Perfect. Just what she needed. A *charity* date to go with the charity event. She grinned at her own witticism. Okay, so her mental play on words hadn't been all that funny. But, then again, neither was this party.

He's ur bro. You have to say that. Does he even know u r trying to set him up on a date?

Not yet. But it'll be fine. And he is cute. Promise.

She hadn't even told him yet. Mila rolled her eyes, thumbs already responding.

That's what u said about the last guy.

She'd let her new friend Freya Rothsberg talk her into going on a different blind date a week ago. That particular man had been good-looking all right, but their date had stalled when he'd road-raged his way down Hollywood Boulevard. She'd ended up hopping out of the car at a stoplight and hailing a cab to take her home.

This is different. PROMISE.

Uh-oh. Her friend had used the word *promise* twice in a row. This time in caps. Never a good sign. Freya was on the other side of the room, waiting for her supposedly gorgeous brother to arrive. Time to head her off at the pass. Maybe she could use humor to soften the blow.

With my luck ur bro is probably short and squatty. A real toad.

The screen stayed blank for almost a minute, and Mila wondered if she'd offended her friend. Then it lit up.

A toad? Really?

A smiley face followed the words. Whew! Not offended.

Yep. T.O.A.D. Warts and all.

Another long pause. Maybe the Wi-Fi reception in the hotel ballroom was glitching or something.

Why don't you look up and see?

Something about those words caused a shiver to ripple across her midsection. Swallowing, she glanced over the top of her screen.

Freya stood right in front of her. Eyes wide. Mouthing something. "I'm sorry."

In that instant, Mila realized her friend was no longer holding a cell phone. Neither was she alone. And the person standing beside her was neither short nor squatty.

Oh. My. God. Her thumbs pretend-typed the words as they sprinted through her head.

The man in the tuxedo was tall. Very tall. And gorgeous?

Yes. Oh, yes. He was also holding something up, turning the object to face her.

A phone—with all Mila's text messages surrounded by a bold blue bubble. The air left her lungs, and she struggled to breathe.

He'd read what she'd written. And suddenly the banter didn't seem quite so innocent. Or funny.

Before she could apologize, one side of the man's mouth tilted up, the movement carving out several craggy lines in his face. If she were a swooner she'd have keeled over by now.

"You know what they say about kissing toads. One of them might just turn out to be a prince."

Her brain fought to process anything other than that low sexy tone. Although she could have sworn the word "kiss" had been in there somewhere. At least, she hoped it had.

She gulped, her eyes straying back to his mouth just as the other side tipped to form a smile that scorched across her senses. If she moved she feared she'd crumple into a pile of ash.

As if reading her thoughts, he passed the phone back to Freya, his gaze never leaving Mila's face. "Shall we test that theory?"

"Th-theory?"

Before she knew what was happening, he'd swept her out onto the dance floor and off her feet. And when his kiss came a few hours later, just as the party was winding down, it was indeed magical. Only there was no need for any kind of transformation. Because James Evan Rothsberg already looked like a prince. A prince whose kiss was every bit as deadly as his smile.

Right then and there Mila knew, without a doubt, her world would never be the same.

CHAPTER ONE

Present day

Bzzzzzz...

No matter how many different ringtones James tried—and it seemed like he'd tried them all—he still hated receiving text messages. The flat sound of his current tone was no different. His pulse sped up and his throat went dry, even though he knew it wasn't from Mila.

Losing the fun, sexy messages they'd used to exchange had been one of the hardest adjustments he'd had to make after calling off the wedding, and his no-texting rule was his way of trying to deal with that.

He shook himself from his stupor. Six years had changed nothing. No matter how right he'd been to break off their engagement, he couldn't blot out the image of the horror in his ex-fiancée's gorgeous hazel eyes when she'd realized it was over.

So were the intimate texts. All texts, in fact, since everyone around him was aware that he preferred actual phone calls to typed messages.

Besides, Mila had taken off to parts unknown soon after he'd skipped out on her, going back to Brazil, where she'd been doing relief work among indigenous people.

Until now.

He'd had a damned good reason for leaving her at the altar: a panicked phone call from a former girlfriend telling him she was pregnant. And an unexpected betrayal by his father.

It didn't matter now that the whole thing had been a setup. That deception had turned out to be a blessing in disguise. Mila had been saved from being dragged into the reality that was his family, with its arguments and its never-ending scandals. His famous parents had been the darlings of the paparazzi for that very reason—even after their divorce years ago.

Mila might not have seen it at the time, but surely in the years since then she'd come to realize the narrow escape she'd had.

He'd never tried to contact her, even after he'd discovered what Cindy had done.

The phone sent him a reminder buzz.

He forced himself to look down at the screen as he exited his car along with the damned photographer the clinic had made him bring along to this meeting. The text was from Freya. The no-text rule had become a running joke with her. She would text him just because she knew how much he hated it. To try to provoke him to answer. It never worked. He always responded with a phone call. Or not at all.

It would seem she was still at it. And under the circumstances it was in extremely poor taste.

We saw you pull up. Waiting just inside.

We. That could only mean one thing. Freya wasn't alone inside that tiny building. Although he'd known she wouldn't be.

Hell. He'd hoped to have a moment or two to get his thoughts together, although he'd had plenty of time to prepare for this photo shoot. Over two months to plan his words down to the final punctuation mark.

Had he done that? No. He had not. Even during the twenty-minute drive out of the more secluded

Hollywood Hills and into the city of Los Angeles itself he'd done no advance planning.

Morgan, the photographer the PR department had contracted, had been more than happy to keep up a steady stream of conversation. She might have been fishing, but James didn't care. He was no longer biting. He was fresh out of yet another superficial relationship, which the paparazzi had followed with glee. He was definitely not ready to test the waters again. Especially not with this meeting with Mila hanging over his head.

He'd avoided thinking about that particular woman. He'd decided that if he kept his head in the sand long enough, this whole damned situation could have just dissolved into nothing.

It hadn't.

And he knew exactly who'd be on the other side of the door once he walked through it.

Mila Brightman.

The woman who'd almost become his wife.

The woman who'd barely escaped that particular fate.

Thank God she had.

He didn't bother to respond to his sister's text. They both knew he was here, so there was no point. How, exactly, his sister had talked him into this arrangement he had no idea. The Hollywood Hills Clinic had been gliding along just fine without another addition to their efficient little family.

Except this was Freya. And Mila. Two women he'd always had trouble saying no to.

Sucking down a resigned breath and dragging a hand through his hair, he waited for Morgan and then he headed up the walk, stopping short when he spied a ragged square of cardboard taped to the outside of one of the clinic's windows. He was so used to the pristine opulence of his own medical center that the squat building huddled on the corner of a busy street seemed as foreign as the relief work Mila had once done. But the sign painted at the top of the clinic was bright and cheery, a bevy of colorful handprints forming an imaginary sidewalk that led to an artist's rendition of the building—only whoever'd painted it had had quite an imagination because although the edifice was the same shape, the painted version was a welcoming place. And there were no cardboard patches in sight.

The photographer raised her camera, aiming it right at the broken window. James wrapped his fingers around the woman's, stopping her short. "No. Not that."

Morgan frowned at him but lowered the camera. "So you only want the positive stuff?"

His eyes were still on the brown square in the window as they reached the front entrance. "That's what we're here for."

Bright Hope Clinic. The painted lettering on the glass door matched the colors of the handprints on the sign. And the glass doors were spotlessly clean. His glance went back to the cardboard patch.

A sliver of unease worked its way through his gut. Not about Mila's safety. Of course not. About the soundness of his decision to allow a branch of this clinic to open inside his own. Freya's doing. Not his. But his damned board of directors had put him in charge of overseeing the opening of the facility. Which was why he was here, pricey photographer in tow.

The woman took a few shots of the sign and the door, dutifully avoiding the window. "We can go inside anytime you want."

Before he could even reach for the door, however, it was flung open and Freya stood there. "Come on, James, what's taking you so long?"

"What happened to the window?" He nodded toward the offending cardboard, not sure he even wanted to know the answer.

Although he couldn't see Mila, she was just inside the dark entrance of the clinic. The growing pressure in his chest told him that. Schooling the rest of his body to mimic the bland mask he wore on his face, he made no move to go inside.

"Oh...um..." Freya glanced behind her. "It's nothing. Probably just a stray baseball."

James turned his attention to the busy street behind him. Cars clogged the asphalt as they waited for the light to change and allow them to head on their way. Baseball? He didn't think so. Not on this road. He lowered his voice, to avoid Morgan hearing him. "Tell me you weren't here when it happened." His sister was seven months pregnant and did not need any stress at this point.

"No, it was sometime last week." She waved off his concern, a frown appearing between her brows.

Biting back his next words, knowing his sister wouldn't welcome any brotherly advice, he sighed, hoping she'd catch his drift.

"It's perfectly safe, James."

Safe? With Mila somewhere inside? He didn't think so.

But he was here. And the sooner he got this over with, the sooner he could be on his way. The space they'd set aside in The Hollywood Hills Clinic was on the other side of the building from where his office was, so it wasn't like he'd see her every day. And he was pretty sure she would split her time between this facility and the new one.

With that bracing thought, he motioned the photographer and Freya inside and then followed them.

The interior of the clinic was as cheerful as the sign. Bright colors were splashed on every available surface, as if a painter had opened his cans and tossed the contents onto the walls and countertops.

"Wow," Morgan said, already snapping shots of the interior.

Wow was right. The place was so very…Mila that it made him smile.

His gaze came back, zeroing in on her at last with a swallow.

Her hair was much longer than it had been when they'd been together. Back then, it had been cropped into short waves above her ears, allowing the delicate bones of her face to shine forth. Not that they didn't still. But unlike the easy-care locks of days past, the new Mila appeared cool and polished, the curls tamed into long sleek strands that ended just below her shoulder blades.

He swallowed again and extended his hand in a fake formality that would make the PR department proud. "Mila, nice to see you again. Thank you for letting the clinic do some publicity shots."

Right on cue, the camera clicked multiple times, reminding him of how often he'd been caught unaware on the streets of LA. During his parents' ugly divorce, he'd barely been able to go anywhere without some member of the paparazzi lying in wait, hoping to get him at the worst possible moment. He tensed, before forcing himself to relax his muscles.

He didn't ask how Mila was doing, and for a split second he thought she'd refuse his greeting. Maybe it would have been better if he'd kept his hands in his pockets, but then she reached forward and curled her fingers around his.

Big mistake. The contact scattered images through his head that were every bit as vivid as the paint on the walls. Memories of Mila's head nestled deep in his pillow as she'd slept, of making love into the early hours. Laughter. Late-night texts. And finally the tears.

Damn it.

As if plagued by the same thoughts, Mila snatched her hand free and turned away. "Nice to see you as well. And it's fine about the publicity. You're used to it by now. Besides, I'm sure your clinic wants to show off its newest investment. So how about a quick tour? I didn't schedule any patients this morning, but you should be able to see—"

He touched her arm to slow the torrent of words. It worked. She swung around, but he noticed she took a step back, the distance just enough that he couldn't touch her again.

"The window. What happened?"

Freya broke in. "James, it's fine. Don't go all protective big brother on us."

Not very likely. The last thing he felt toward

Mila was brotherly affection. But he did feel a niggle of worry.

He narrowed his eyes on his sister. "I think we have a right to know the risks involved in taking on this little venture."

He glanced toward Morgan, but she was ignoring them, still exploring the waiting room, where brightly colored plastic chairs perched on top of acid-stained concrete that had been polished until it gleamed.

"*Little* venture?" If Mila's voice had been cool before, it had now dropped to well below freezing. "Afraid you might lose some of your high-dollar clients if they spot a pair of humble flip-flops cruising down the fancy halls of your clinic?"

His jaw tightened. Not at her words but at the disdain in her tone. And the fact that she had hit a nerve. The board had discussed at length how to handle their newest addition.

The voting members had made a motion to add a separate entrance so that Bright Hope could be accessed directly from the parking lot, instead of its patients coming in through the huge double doors at the front of the clinic. The decision stuck in his craw because putting in another door made it seem a little too much like a service entrance for comfort.

He'd gone along with it only because if he hadn't, the vote to allow the opening of the clinic might not have gone through—and Freya had her heart set on it. It had only passed by a slim margin as it was. And the financially challenged kids of LA did need access to what The Hollywood Hills Clinic could offer.

Telling Mila any of that, however, would not make her feel any better. If he knew her, she had only agreed to Freya's idea because his sister had insisted.

Which meant Bright Hope was not doing as well financially as she had made it seem.

"Let's just say we'd rather not have a gang war break out in one of our hallways."

Mila's eyes flitted sideways away from his.

Damn. He'd been joking about the gang war. Had that broken window been caused by a hail of bullets? "Do you have security?"

"Yes. There are cameras, and a security guard is here during business hours."

But only during those hours. Did Mila come here when there was no one else around? The question tickled the back of his throat, but he ignored it. He didn't want Morgan going back to the board with any tales that weren't true. He took another tack instead.

"Did the police catch whoever broke your window?"

"Not yet, but I've turned the surveillance video over to them. Hopefully they'll find the culprits."

Culprits, plural. "Do you keep drugs on the premises?"

She threw him a stormy glare that he recognized all too well. "Of course not. Nothing stronger than over-the-counter pain medication. There's a pharmacy around the corner, if we need something stronger."

That was smart. "Was anything taken?"

"They didn't try to gain entry."

Strange. Maybe she was right. Maybe it had just been a stray ball from a kid.

And from her curt answer, that was all he was going to get out of her. "Well, then, let's take that tour, so Morgan can shoot some pictures, and I'll let you get back to whatever you were doing."

"So she *does* have a name." His ex-fiancée

leaned closer with an amused smile, one brow raised.

What was that supposed to mean?

Oh, hell. He'd seen the women shake hands but he'd forgotten to introduce them. Bad manners on his part, but he didn't exactly think straight when Mila was around.

Well, even if she thought there was something going on between him and the photographer, who cared? She'd been dating Tyler, that brawny firefighter, until recently, hadn't she?

With the same fixed smile, Mila indicated for them to follow her down a small hallway to an exam room.

This space was decorated in tropical island hues. Ocean-blue walls and sand-colored linoleum were a smart choice. As was the artist's rendition of a palm tree painted in the corner. The same beige from the flooring flowed up onto the bottom half of the wall, meandering across it, giving the lone tree a place to root and thrive. Individual grains glimmered under the overhead lights, much as they would beneath the sun. A few painted conches dotted the surface of this imaginary beach.

All in all, it was a tropical paradise any child would love and not a cold, sterile exam room. This was a place of adventure, not of fear and pain. And as skillful as Morgan might be, there was no way she was going to capture the feel of this room.

He wandered over and ran a finger across the textured paint that made up one of the palm fronds. "This is pretty amazing, Mila."

Maybe they should incorporate some of these designs in the new clinic to tie the two centers together. It would be a little different from the posh chrome and Italian marble in the rest of The Hollywood Hills Clinic, but maybe that would be a good thing. It might even give the board a reason to rethink having a separate entrance for Bright Hope. And it would make Mila feel more comfortable with her surroundings.

He knew firsthand she didn't like over-the-top extravagance. She'd practically cringed every time she'd had to get into his car six years ago.

It highlighted one of the biggest differences between them. Orphaned as a child, when her parents had been killed during a home invasion, Mila had been left a huge inheritance by her famous

Hollywood parents. But she didn't live like it. In fact, she gave her money away whenever she got the chance. James, on the other hand, enjoyed the security that money could buy. Security he hadn't felt during his childhood years, even though his parents had been just as wealthy as Mila's, if not more so.

He gritted his teeth until his thoughts were back under control.

Surely by now even Mila could see that he'd done her a favor by breaking off their engagement. They'd been doomed, even without Cindy's deceit.

"Can we get some pictures of the three of you in front of that mural?" Morgan asked.

Freya gave a horrified snort. "Oh, no. Not me, thank you very much. I'm about to pop, and I'd rather not do it in front of a camera." She threw her brother a look. "You and Mila should be in it, since you represent what this partnership is all about. It would be good to have some publicity shots of you two, anyway."

Why the hell hadn't he thought of the possibility of having to cozy up to his ex in some of the pictures? Because he'd figured Freya would be in them as well.

Nothing to do but get it over with. He gestured for Mila to go ahead of him. She hesitated for several long seconds, then her shoulders dropped in resignation and she trudged over to the mural. James moved in as well, standing a good five feet away from her.

"Can you move closer?" Morgan waved her hand. "You're blocking part of the tree."

Was it his imagination, or did the photographer have a slightly "gotcha" smirk to her expression? Maybe he should have been a little less standoffish when she'd been flirting with him in the car because right now it looked like she was enjoying having him at her mercy.

He took a couple of steps to the left, trying to talk his way through his discomfort. "Who did your paint job? It might not be a bad idea to match this look in the new clinic."

She didn't get a chance to answer, because Freya grinned. "Mila did it. She painted the clinic signs as well. Aren't they great?"

His sister's pride was evident. As was the warning gleam in her eyes that told him not to say anything that would hurt Mila's feelings. As if he would.

The photographer snapped a couple of pictures right as that news was relayed. Even he could feel the shock on his face. He hated to think what it would come across as on film.

He glanced back to get a closer look at the tree. It was good. Very good. Right down to the smooth green of the coconuts hanging from it. He could have sworn she'd had it done by a professional. But then again she had lived in the tropics of Brazil so it made sense that she would have had learned to improvise and do more than practice medicine. And she had always loved children.

A trait that seemed to be missing from his family tree.

Another area of incompatibility. If only he'd been looking at their relationship with a clinical eye six years ago, he would have seen it. It had taken a shock from an ex-girlfriend and an offer of payment from his dad to make him see the reality of what Mila would be subjected to if he married her.

Another flash of Morgan's camera, but he was too busy with his thoughts to take much notice.

Mila had survived. Improvised.

Had she improvised with some Brazilian man after he'd broken things off with her?

A thought he had no business dwelling on.

"Can you both turn toward the front? I'd like a couple more in this room before we move on."

They both swiveled on their heels and faced the photographer.

"So do you think you can replicate this over at my clinic?" he asked.

She threw him a glance, the brow from earlier edging back up. "Beaches and palm trees won't exactly match the theme you have going on over there, would it? What do you call it, by the way? Moneyed Green? Or are you just hoping artwork like this will highlight the differences between your clinic and mine—your patients and mine?"

The camera went off again.

Damn the woman. A muscle in his jaw clenched. "I was trying to pay Bright Hope a compliment. Forget I asked."

Fingers landed on his forearm, and her eyes closed for a second before reopening. "I'm sorry, James, that was inexcusable of me. Can we start over?"

It was far too late for that. But if cold indifference was the way she wanted to play this game, then she would find he could match her, ice chip for ice chip. Except she'd never been an ice queen. Far from it. In fact, he'd always liked Mila's hot temperament. It had matched the places she'd been. Stoked his own internal fires.

But he'd better figure out how to extinguish that particular flamethrower. And soon. First, though, he had to get rid of that damned camera, which seemed to be recording their every expression.

She'd almost blown things. As Mila gave James and his photographer the grand tour, and it wasn't much, with the tiny size of her clinic and the money crunch they'd been under for the last few months, she tried her best not to let her animosity toward him show any more than it already had. Six years after the fact, she should be over their breakup. But his comment about her decorating choices had made it fizz up like the head on a beer. And he hadn't even meant it as a cut.

She drew in a deep breath. It was up to her to calm the waters.

Only how was she supposed to do that when the waters churning inside her were gray and choppy?

And with that photographer giving him the eye for most of the visit?

She pushed open the door at the far end of the hall. "And this is our business office."

The head of her young assistant, Avery Phelps, popped up from behind her rickety desk, her brown eyes widening. She backed out of the narrow space on her hands and knees and climbed to her feet, tugging the hem of her blouse down over her tanned midriff. "Hey, Mi. Sorry. I was just trying to get this stupid cord to stay in place for once."

"The computer again?"

"Yes. And I lost an hour's worth of work this time."

Mila groaned as she glanced at the empty screen of the computer monitor. "I'm so sorry. I keep meaning to have someone come out and take a look." It was still weird to her to have to rely on technology to keep up with things when she was used to taking patient notes on actual paper, with an actual writing instrument. She preferred jotting things down, it seemed more personal.

But she couldn't ask Avery to do that when things in the US were all done via computer. The young woman had been with Mila from the very beginning, when she'd rushed into Bright Hope as the frantic single mom of a very ill three-year-old girl. It had turned out Sarah had type one diabetes. Once they'd gotten her blood-sugar level under control, Avery had wanted to give something back and had insisted on donating several hours a week to the clinic—after working her own full-time job. She'd been at Bright Hope ever since, eventually becoming an employee rather than just a volunteer, and Mila had no idea what she'd do without the woman.

"Do you want me to take a look at it?" James's voice rumbled over their heads.

Yeah, it would have been pretty tempting to ask him to crawl around underneath that desk, but she was afraid her body would go haywire and send out pheromonal signals that could be detected for miles. "It's just a loose power cord but every time the desk jiggles, the power blinks in and out, and Avery loses data."

He gave the old machine a dubious look. "Not good for your system. Do you have any tape?"

"Tried that a couple of times." She was proud of herself for being one step ahead of him. Although it was really Avery who had thought of that. And how embarrassing was it to have this exchange in front of a camera?

"How about surgical tape? Or even phlebotomy tubing?"

How was that supposed to work any better than what they'd already tried?

Before she could ask, Avery said, "I'll get you some. Anything to keep the darned thing going."

Mila made a mental note to get someone techy out to look at the machine. The last thing she wanted was for James to have to come out to fix things.

Like her practice itself? If Freya hadn't gotten him to agree to pump some funds into Bright Hope and allow her to open a branch inside The Hollywood Hills Clinic, people like Avery would have very few options. Mila had gone through most of her inheritance in the years since her aunt had passed away. Not that she missed the money. She didn't. But she missed what it could do.

Within a minute her assistant had come back with a roll of latex tube tourniquet and wide surgical tape. "Pick your poison." Avery said it with a smile, but a shiver went over Mila. Maybe because her poison had been James once upon a time. And like a slow-acting toxin, he'd killed the part of her heart that she'd handed over to his care.

"Let's try the tubing first."

Freya, who'd been silently watching the exchange, smiled. "My brother the handyman. Always trying to fix what's broken."

Was her friend talking about the eating disorder she'd overcome years ago? Mila remembered James's sometimes heavy-handed tactics when it came to his sister, but Freya said that things had mellowed between them over the last year or so. Especially now that she and Zack had fallen in love and gotten married. Their twins were weeks away from being born, and the pair was ecstatic. Mila had done her best to be happy for her friend, but it struck too close to home. That could have been her and James had he not decided that a wife whose passion was working with various relief organizations would cramp his Hollywood style.

That might not be exactly true, but something had given him cold feet. He knew she wasn't interested in being a big earner, so she'd always assumed that had had something to do with it. Only James had never seen fit to tell her why he hadn't wanted to marry her. Just that she was better off without him.

And she was.

Definitely.

And he could keep his reasons for breaking their engagement to himself. After all, she was used to being kept in the dark. Her aunt had loved her, but in trying to protect her she'd left Mila unprepared for the shocking reality of her parents' deaths. They hadn't died in a car accident, like her aunt had told her. In fact, her mother had lingered for days in a hospital after being shot. Ten-year-old Mila had never even had the chance say goodbye. It had taken her a long time to forgive her aunt for that once she'd discovered the truth.

The Mila of today did not believe in holding back information no matter how unpalatable or difficult it might be. To do so was to destroy her trust. So James's refusal to level with her had made it easy for her to walk away and never look back.

His voice came from nowhere, jerking her back to the present.

"I'll need some scissors." He tested the flexibility of the tubing he'd been handed.

What was he going to do with it?

Avery grabbed a pair of sharp scissors from the desk and handed them over.

Somehow wedging his large body between the leg of the desk and the wall, he grunted a quick oath at something and then remained silent for several minutes.

And the view from where she was standing was exquisite.

A length of tubing appeared on one side of the computer. "Can you grab that, Mila?"

Conscious of the pencil skirt she'd donned for the photo shoot, and praying the photographer didn't catch a wardrobe malfunction, she knelt down and took hold of the tubing that he'd pushed beside the computer. Only it now had a dark stain on it. Red. Wet.

"Are you bleeding?"

She glanced up at Avery, who read her wordless request. Within a second or two she handed Mila a bottle of hand sanitizer and some gauze. She quickly wiped down the tubing and lobbed another question toward James. "What's going on back there?"

"Tie it at the front of the computer."

She frowned. How was this supposed to fix anything? "How tight do you want it?"

"Pull it taut and then start the computer up."

Mila tied the two ends together and made a quick knot in the rubber. "Okay, let's see if that did it."

Pushing the start button, the screen leapt to life, along with a warning that the computer hadn't shut down correctly.

"No kidding," her assistant muttered, staring at the monitor.

"It's going, James. Thank you."

A few seconds later the man edged backward and climbed to his feet. The fingers of his right hand were pressed tightly against the sleeve of his dress shirt, where another stain had formed. "Oh, my God, what did you do?"

A series of clicks went off behind them. Mila ignored the sound.

"It's nothing. Just found some old tack strip along the wall."

Oh, no. The building had been carpeted when they'd first moved in. Mila had immediately gone to work removing it and then prying up the tack strip. By the end of the process she'd been dog tired, and since the office desk had always been there, she'd left the lone strip where it was. She'd forgotten all about it until now. It was a wonder Avery hadn't cut herself on it. She threw the woman a look. "I'm sorry, I totally forgot about it."

Her assistant gave her arm a gentle squeeze. "It's fine. I've never had any problems avoiding it."

Avery was a lot smaller than James, so that was probably true. Still, it didn't make her feel any better.

"Let me see." She held her hand toward him. He eyed her for a second and then shook his head.

"It's nothing. Just a scratch."

"Then you won't mind if I look at it."

His jaw tightened, but he didn't argue with her again. He let her take his hand. The second his skin touched hers, a frisson of awareness trickled up her arm and circled her chest. She did her best to beat it back, turning his hand over to get a better look at it.

The flash of a camera went off in the background, making her suddenly aware that Morgan had been snapping away as nobody had told her not to. The last thing Mila wanted was a shot with her and James holding hands. But if she said something, he would know, so instead she found the spot where he'd cut himself. Long jagged lines ran parallel to his little finger, going up the side of his hand. Nasty looking but not deep enough to need stitches. "Have you had a tetanus shot recently?"

James's brows went up. "Yes."

Of course he had. He was a doctor. Her face burned, but she forced her voice to remain steady. "Avery, would you mind getting me some more gauze, please? And some alcohol from the cabinet in the exam room?"

The photographer slid sideways, her camera still up to her eye as she snapped shot after shot.

Evidently James had had enough. "I think you've taken enough pictures, Morgan, don't you?"

Whether he didn't want their picture to pop up in the society pages with speculation about them rekindling their past romance or something else, his low words had their desired effect. The woman murmured something that might have been either thanks or an apology and put her camera back around her neck. She then glanced at her watch. "Oops. I'm late for my next appointment. I'll just grab a taxi, if you don't mind. Thank you, though, for letting me hitch a ride to the clinic."

James nodded, but said nothing. Freya offered to see her out.

The pair left, leaving Mila alone with her ex.

"Nice touch," he said, indicating the hand she still held.

"Excuse me?"

"The clinic has been trying to improve my image. Evidently my bedside manner isn't always as soft and cuddly as the board would like it to be."

A thought came to her. "Did you cut yourself on purpose?"

"No." He nodded at their joined hands. "Did you do *that* on purpose?"

She released him. "Of course not. I was just trying to help."

His gaze came up to spear hers. "And so was I."

There was something about the way he said that that made her... No. It had nothing to do with their past.

She squared her shoulders. "And you are. Thank you." She gestured toward the computer. "For that, and for convincing The Hollywood Hills Clinic to take on Bright Hope."

"It'll be good for our image."

All of the warm feelings that had bubbled up a few moments earlier popped, leaving her feeling oddly flat. "I'm sure it will."

"Hey." He slid the fingers of his uninjured hand beneath her chin. "I didn't mean it like that. I meant it would be good for my clinic's image… and for yours. Your patients will know they're going to get quality care."

He cut off the words before she could say them. "Not that they wouldn't be getting that at this location, but we will lend you instant credibility. You might not like what that brings with it, though. Prepare to be inundated."

If he was trying to scare her, it wasn't working. She'd been swamped with patients plenty of times. In fact, the more she worked, the less she thought of her sad lack of a personal life, and how poor Tyler had pressed and pressed for a decision about taking their relationship to the next level, to the point she'd finally had to break things off with him. She couldn't do to him what had been done to her. And she'd at least had the guts to hand him the truth rather than dish up a halfhearted fabrication.

Like her aunt had about her parents' deaths?

Or was she thinking of James and the way he'd ended things?

"Don't worry about me," she said. "I can handle just about anything."

Avery came back into the room with the items she'd asked for, and Mila hurriedly cleaned up James's hand with the alcohol, although he waved aside the need for any kind of bandage. "It would just get in my way."

"Are you sure?"

"Yes." He glanced at her face. "I'll let you know when the photos come back so you can look through them."

Good. That way she could weed out the ones that made her and James look a little too friendly toward each other.

Because things between them were anything but friendly.

And if she was smart, she would keep it that way. Despite the fact that they were going to be seeing a lot more of each other in the future, she would have to protect her heart. Because James had already hurt her once. She had to make sure he never got the chance to do so again.

CHAPTER TWO

DINNER PROBABLY WASN'T the best place to do this.

But it wasn't like he wanted these photos flashed around the corridors of The Hollywood Hills Clinic. At least, not all of them. Which begged the question of why he hadn't just tossed the more questionable pictures.

Why? Because he didn't trust his own judgment, that's why. He could be seeing things that weren't there. Things that were remnants of days gone by. Maybe Mila would glance through them and not bat an eye. It wasn't like there was anything suggestive about them.

They just looked…cozy. Not a word he would use to describe their current relationship.

Strained. Awkward. Difficult. Those were much more accurate terms. And if Mila didn't desperately need the funding that his medical center could provide, he had no doubt she would have refused to work with him in the first place.

All of this was because of Freya.

He eyed the entry plaque of the Très Magnifique with its gold-plated edging for the fifth time. Still no sign of his dinner date. He had always been punctual to the point of an obsession, while Mila had taken on the characteristics of the Brazilian people she'd worked with over the years. With them it was about relationships and not about the hands on a clock.

And exactly which relationship was she culti-vating this time? The one with that firefighter she used to date? Was she seeing him again? If so, what did the man think of his girlfriend going out to dinner with a former lover?

It wasn't dinner. It was a business date.

And yet it made his skin chill to think of Mila as anyone's girlfriend. But he'd given up the right to that title—or the title of fiancé—a long time ago. One stupid lie had changed everything. And it hadn't even been his lie. But that, combined with his father's dark suggestion, had made him rethink the direction his life had been taking.

Everything with Mila had happened so fast, a flare-up of emotions he'd never realized he'd had.

But Mila was all about family and helping those

in need. Maybe because her parents had died, and she'd been left alone.

Family, unfortunately, was the exact thing James hoped to avoid. His own family had been a disaster. Between the tabloids, the violent arguments and his father's very real infidelities James had always been leery of steady relationships. Then Mila had come along, and he hadn't been able to resist anything about her. For the first time he'd started thinking about forever.

Until Cindy and his father had destroyed the fairy tale. And that's all it had been. Mila had never tried to contact him once he'd ended things. Never really tried to ask why he'd backed out of their wedding at the last minute.

If she'd truly loved him, wouldn't she have wanted to probe a little deeper? Instead, she'd accepted his "it just won't work between us...we want different things out of life" explanation at face value.

"Sorry to keep you waiting." The breathless voice rushing toward him brought the gavel down on his thoughts.

Tightening his hold on the attaché case he carried, he turned to look at her. The fact that the first place his gaze parked was her lips, looking for any signs that she'd been kissed recently, irritated him. He focused on what time it was instead. "I see some things never change."

That soft mouth he'd been staring at tightened in warning. "I had a patient."

Damn. She was a doctor. Why had the possibility she'd gotten delayed due to a case never crossed his mind?

Maybe for the same reason that he saw coy glances passing between them in those pictures.

And she was only six minutes late. It only felt like he'd been waiting for her forever.

Hell, he remembered thinking almost those exact same words at their first meeting. The one where she'd called him a toad.

Unfortunately for Mila, he'd never really perfected the transformation into a prince. And she'd discovered far too late that she should have bypassed kissing him altogether.

Except he hadn't given her much of a choice, insisting that she dance with him.

Forcing himself to come back to the present, he motioned toward the door. "They're holding our table for us. Shall we?"

Mila glanced at the sign, and then the hand-carved door, her teeth catching her lower lip.

Had she been here before?

Not likely. This wasn't the kind of place the Mila he'd known would have frequented. So why had he brought her here?

The hostess guided them through the front part of the fancy establishment, and James tensed as his glance trailed over Mila's formfitting dress and the staccato twitch of her hips as she followed the woman. She didn't generally like dressing up, and when she'd heard the name of the restaurant there'd been a long pause over the phone before she'd finally accepted the invitation.

Now that they were here, he realized he should have made sure the restaurant knew this was a business dinner and nothing more—because the employee was taking them back to the table he was normally seated at when he dined here: a secluded spot in the very corner, away from prying eyes…and cameras.

He probably should have chosen a different place to eat. But they knew him here and it was generally easier to get a last-minute reservation than at the places where celebrities normally hung out.

There were some of those at Très Magnifique as well, but the dim lighting, specially coated glass and tight security made it hard for the paparazzi to gain access to its patrons. Another reason why this was one of his go-to restaurants.

The distaste of having his face splashed across the tabloids was a holdover from his childhood, when his parents' every move had made the front pages. James had seen his own mistakes—including his broken engagement—paraded for all the world to see. Because of that, he'd become adept at avoiding the places those kinds of photographers frequented.

Mila slid into her seat, setting her small clutch purse on a corner of the table. "I assume you have them with you."

He had to smile at the way she lowered her voice, since it mirrored some of his own thoughts. Leaning forward, he mimicked her hushed tones.

"Yes. I have them. They're in my briefcase. But I think you went into the wrong line of work, Mi."

"Come again?"

"You should have been a spy."

Her lips went up as well. "Am I being too paranoid about this whole thing?"

A possible reason for her behavior slid up from somewhere inside him. He didn't know if she'd started seeing someone else since breaking up with Tyler, but it was a possibility. Or maybe they'd even gotten back together. "Will this be a problem for your boyfriend? I'd be happy to call him and explain, if you'd like." Although the last thing he wanted to do was call Mila's boyfriend and tell him this meeting was purely platonic.

Not when the last thing he wanted it to be was platonic.

Not with her sitting across from him in a dark green dress that hugged her form and showed just a touch of creamy curves at the neckline. Curves he'd once explored at his leisure. He forced his eyes back to her face, noting she was biting her lip again.

What the hell? Had she gone and gotten engaged or something? His stomach sank like a rock.

"No. You don't need to explain anything."

Because this guy, unlike him, would need no explanation as to why Mila was dining with her ex-fiancé? If she were still *his*, he sure as hell would have wanted to know why she was having dinner with another man. Especially since she was a physician and not a CEO, which meant there was no need to dine with clients.

"He must trust you." He forced the words to sound impartial.

"It's not that." She toyed with the clasp of her purse for a second or two. "I'm not seeing anyone. I told you I'd broken up with Tyler."

She had told him. But people changed their minds.

James stared at her for some clue as to what might have gone wrong between them.

"It was me," she continued. "This time."

Said as if she needed him to know that James wasn't the only one capable of backing out of an unwanted relationship.

"I'm sorry."

Sorry for the way he'd treated her? Or that his past actions might be affecting the way she navigated current-day relationships?

"Don't be. I don't believe in stringing someone along when I know how the story is going to end."

The barb sank deep. Because that's exactly what he had done to Mila. Strung her along, even when he'd known that he was eventually going to break things off. Both because of Cindy and the bombshell she'd dropped, and because of his own father's response to it. He couldn't follow in the award-winning actor and egotistical bastard's footsteps. He would not father a child that he would be no good at nurturing. Or throw money at the mother of that child to make the whole thing go away. So James had done neither, deciding to break it off with Mila and do the right thing by Cindy. Only it had all been a lie.

Mila's dreamy words the last time they'd slept together about starting a family had hit him at the worst possible moment. Their courtship had been such a whirlwind affair that children had never been discussed. And then Cindy had dropped her bombshell and almost immediately afterward Mila had wistfully expressed her own desire for children.

His reaction had confirmed what he'd believed about himself all along: that he truly was like his celebrity parents, who had left him and Freya to the mercy of a string of nannies. He was no nurturer.

Even his attempts at standing in for his parents when it came to his sister had ended in disaster. He'd been overbearing and overprotective. In some ways he blamed himself for the eating disorder Freya had developed, wondering if it was because he'd been too controlling about what she did…who she went out with. He sure hadn't practiced what he'd preached back then, because he'd gone out with scads of women who'd meant nothing to him. Including Cindy.

Hell, he'd been the worst possible role model for her.

His regrets over his mistakes with Freya and the scare of that unplanned pregnancy with Cindy had given him a fear of having children of his own. It had gotten so bad that he had stopped treating children in his medical practice, referring them instead to colleagues. Which had left him treating insipid socialites and celebrities. People very much like his parents—a peck on each cheek, a little nip, a little tuck, and they were good to go.

Only he'd grown tired of it all. Weary in a way that he didn't understand.

"Drinks, sir?"

He blinked back to the present as the server handed them each a menu.

Maybe Mila had been lost in her own thoughts as well because she wasn't staring at him like he had two heads. He waited as she asked for a glass of wine, and then he did the same, adding an order of stuffed mushrooms—something he remembered her loving. Although why he felt the need to do anything other than toss the pictures across the table and eat a quick bite was beyond him. Except he probably wasn't going to get to sit across a table from Mila Brightman ever again. And maybe a part of him wanted to relive the days he'd left behind. Now that he knew she didn't have someone waiting at home for her, that urge had grown stronger.

The server left to get their drinks, and Mila propped her elbows on the table, staring at him. "So how does this work, exactly?"

He frowned. Had she read his thoughts? The idea of taking up where they'd left off flashed through his head. Somehow he doubted that's what she meant.

"How does what work?"

"The pictures. Do you want me to look through them before we eat? Or after we're done? Just how bad are they that we're even sitting here?"

Ah…so she had realized something was up when he'd asked her out to dinner. "They're not bad. I just…"

He hadn't expected to have to explain his reasoning. He tried again. "I just thought we should go through them without an audience. That might be hard at the clinic or even at Bright Hope."

Especially with a few of the more intimate shots. And Morgan had seemed to be quite adept at catching them at just the wrong moment. A woman scorned who was doing her best to embarrass him? Or was it inevitable that he would see the pictures through a different filter than other people?

Mila's lips curved. "Did she catch you crawling under that desk or something? I can see how you might want to hide that particular shot."

He laughed. "I take it the view wasn't all that flattering from where you were standing."

"Let's just say it was interesting."

Interesting.

He couldn't be sure with the low lighting in the restaurant, but he thought maybe a bit of color had seeped into her cheeks, and he couldn't help but follow this trail just a little further. Especially since he could picture several office desk scenarios he wouldn't have minded exploring once upon a time. "Interesting good? Or interesting bad?"

"I think the photographer thought it was good, that's for sure."

Had Mila noticed the other woman's interest? He thought he'd made it pretty clear that she was there on a professional basis only. He hadn't been interested.

"And you. What did you think?" Okay, so this was pursuing it a little too far.

"I think maybe we should stick to the subject at hand."

Not exactly a denial. More like an evasion. Which meant maybe he wasn't the only one who was struggling to keep their old relationship where it belonged: firmly in the past. But he'd better make more of an effort, or he was going to find himself in a very uncomfortable place.

"Fair enough. Why don't we sort through them now, then?"

Mila swallowed as she shuffled through the sheaf of glossy photos that James had brought out of his leather attaché case. Now she saw why he'd wanted to bring her to a place where the tables were private and the lights were low.

Even with the dim lighting in the restaurant

these shots made something in her belly come to life. These were not the kind of publicity pictures one wanted for the grand opening of a charity clinic. At least, not some of them.

One of the photos in front of the mural did more than light a fire in her gut. It made her face heat. Because she and James were gazing at each other, and while she couldn't exactly read his expression, hers was filled with dread—with a side order of longing. A longing that had made one of her hands stretch toward him a bit? Coaxing him to move closer to her like Morgan had asked? Lord, she hoped not.

Maybe she was simply gesturing toward something in the mural. But she didn't think so.

She flipped through a couple more, and then paused once again. James was watching her as she said something to Avery, a slight smile on his face, hands stuffed in the pockets of his dress slacks. He looked so endearingly at ease that it made her chest ache. It was as if she'd been sucked through a time warp and was looking through a window to the past.

Their past.

She could remember glancing toward him and

catching him with this exact same expression. As if he loved watching her go about life.

Swallowing, she looked up at him. "Is there anything in here that can be salvaged?"

She had no idea if there was a software program invented that could change these pictures into something they weren't. And it made her feel a little queasy that the emotions she felt on the inside were so very visible on the outside. At least in these shots.

But then again, hadn't Morgan caught James off guard in them as well?

"Some of them aren't as bad. But I wanted us to decide that together."

"I can see why."

Their server returned with their appetizers and wine. Mila handed the photos back to James for safekeeping. Or was it simply so she didn't have to look at them anymore this evening? She had a thought. "Maybe you can come to Bright Hope once we finish up here and we can spread them out on the reception desk."

"That sounds like a plan. Speaking of Bright Hope, did you get the glass in that window replaced?"

"Yes, someone came the day after your visit. It's as good as new."

"No other attempted break-ins?"

She paused in cutting one of her mushrooms. "It was just an accident. The police seem to think so as well."

Was it her imagination, or had James just relaxed in his seat? Maybe. She knew how relieved she'd been when the officers had said it looked like a rock kicked up by a car or something. There had been construction on that street not so very long ago.

Popping the morsel into her mouth and chewing, she studied the changes in James over the past six years. His hair seemed even more golden than it had before. From spending time in the California sun?

He'd once been an avid sailor, his sleek schooner making the trek back and forth to Catalina Island every chance he'd had. Hours on his boat would explain his deep tan. And she loved the way the crinkles at the corners of his eyes were lighter than the surrounding skin, as if he smiled more while out on the water than he did at other times. He had when they'd been together, anyway.

She swallowed, trying to nip her speculations in the bud. It was none of her business what he did or didn't do. Not anymore.

"What are you thinking about?"

Time to scramble. She didn't dare stray too far from the truth, because he'd read it in her face if she told him a complete lie. "Do you still go out on the water?"

One side of his mouth twisted into a half smile. "Every chance I get."

"On the *Mystic Waters*?"

His smile slid away this time. "Yes, I still have her. I can't imagine giving her up for anything."

Unlike Mila, who he'd been able to give up with a snap of his fingers. It stung to know that his boat had been with him longer than she had. Since they'd actually spent quite a bit of time on the schooner during their romance, the images it brought up were unbearably intimate. For all her discomfort about displays of wealth, the boat was one place she'd felt at home. Maybe because James had gone to great lengths to put her at ease.

It normally took four hours to sail from Los Angeles to the port of Avalon on the island of Catalina, but it had often taken them even longer, because James would stop every time she'd squealed in delight over some new sight, whether it had been porpoises trying to catch a ride on the boat's wake, or something else. And when he'd taken her below…

Her eyes shut for a second or two before reopening and finding him watching her.

He knew. Knew exactly what she was picturing. Damn him!

"The boats I spent my time on were a little different from your schooner."

"Rubbing my nose in the fact that you've given back more to humanity than I have?"

No. She wasn't. And she had no idea why she'd spouted off like some self-righteous prig. Maybe because it still hurt to know how easily he could toss her aside.

It seemed like every time she'd trusted someone, they'd broken her heart. Her aunt. The men she'd dated in the past. James.

His betrayal had been the worst of all of them.

But he'd gone to bat for her with the board of directors at The Hollywood Hills Clinic. That meant something. He might have founded the medical center, but that didn't mean he made all its decisions. Still, his support was probably the main reason they'd deigned to back a joint venture with Bright Hope.

Freya, as part-owner of the clinic, had helped push it through, she had no doubt. But James was the driving force, the one who'd made sure it happened. Who'd helped make sure disadvantaged children and their parents got the help they needed.

And the fact that she'd just wiped any trace of a smile off his face made her feel sick. When had she turned into such a shrew?

Bracing herself for the impact, she set her fork down and reached across to touch his hand.

"You've given back plenty, James. I remember you working on that little boy whose face had been damaged in that car—"

"I don't do that kind of work anymore." If anything, his jaw tightened even more. "I've gone back to traditional practice, leaving post-traumatic facial reconstruction to…other doctors."

She sat back in her seat, shock washing over her. He was a gifted plastic surgeon so traditional practice had to mean that he…

She truly was a fool. A fool who'd once hoped

James would join her on her treks to other countries, helping those who'd been disfigured, either through birth or through some kind of violent act. So had he only pretended to be interested in those things?

Evidently. Until he'd lost interest in her. Those long intimate conversations about the future and the good they could do together had meant nothing.

Nothing.

So why had he even tried to help Bright Hope get a foothold in the Los Angeles community and beyond?

It had to be because of Freya.

Mila had allowed herself to hope that maybe… just maybe James remembered their time together fondly and had used the funding from his clinic to show her that.

The waiter had set their dinner plates in front of them at some point, without Mila really paying attention to anything except James. The thought of eating now made her gut churn.

Maybe he read something in her face. Maybe he'd just realized how his words had sounded, because he leaned forward a bit, snagging her gaze with his.

"I'm happy about what you do, Mila. Glad there are still people like you in the world." A muscle in his throat worked. "I'm just not one of them. Those cases, they…"

He shook his head, not finishing his sentence.

"They bother you?"

Was that it? He couldn't bear to look at what humans could do to each other?

"Yes. They bother me." And this time Mila swore she saw a glimmer of something in his face. Compassion. Or maybe anger. She really couldn't tell. But it beat that blank mask he tended to wear.

Except for in those pictures. Then it had slipped when she wasn't looking. The camera had been watching, though, and it had caught him in the act.

Only Mila had no idea what any of it meant.

"They bother me too, James, but someone has to help them."

"I know." He lifted a shoulder. "It just can't be me. Not anymore."

"Why?"

The muscle in his jaw went back to its rhythmic pulse. "I'm just not cut out for it. I do better with the celebrities and socialites, like my parents. We come from the same world. We understand each other."

She shook her head. "I don't believe that."

"Believe it. It's true." He picked up his fork and cut into his thick slab of steak. "Don't let your food get cold. Très Magnifique does a wonderful job."

Mila had ordered beef tips with mushrooms over pasta. Spearing a bite-sized piece of meat, she tried to figure out what was going on with him. Only she was no good at reading this man. Not anymore. Maybe not even when they'd been together, since she'd been so sure he'd been as happy as she had.

Except he hadn't been. Not toward the end. He'd been pulling away, and she'd found herself becoming something she hadn't liked. A grasping, frightened girl, trying to do her best to hold a fading romance together all by herself.

Never again.

She would never throw her heart back into the ring like she had during her time with James. Tyler had known the score and had been willing to wait for her to trust him fully. When she'd realized she'd never be able to give him what he needed, she'd broken it off.

And she missed his friendship. Especially now. Especially when confronted with a man who still had the power to wound her with the tiniest of barbs.

Like his unwillingness to work on those who so desperately needed his skills?

Yes.

But there'd been something behind his words. His relationship with his parents had always been rocky at best. And at the very end, when he'd broken off their engagement, he'd said something about his father. The loathing in his voice would have shocked her under normal circumstances but the agony she'd felt in realizing their relationship was over had drowned any other thoughts for a very long time.

Had the man threatened to cut James from his will for marrying a shy do-gooder who shunned the celebrity scene?

Somehow she couldn't picture James caring one way or the other. He'd made his own way in the world, his wealthy clientele willing to pay exorbitant prices to be ensconced in the luxury and prestige of his clinic and be catered to by some of the best physicians in the world. From cardiac surgery to face-lifts, from cradle to geriatrics, the medical center gave the finest care available.

She'd never understood what had happened between them, other than she hadn't been enough to make him happy. And she'd been too angry to ask if his surface explanation—that they weren't right for each other—was the truth. After discovering what her aunt had done, she'd decided she was never going to try to pry the truth out of anyone ever again. They could either tell her or not, but if they chose the latter, she was done with them.

Forcing herself to swallow, she pasted a smile on her face. "Thank you. You were right, the meal was delicious." Not that she'd actually tasted much of it beyond the first few bites. "I'm ready whenever you are."

"Would you like coffee?"

She hesitated. James had always liked to finish his meal with a nice strong java, no matter what the time. Caffeine had never seemed to affect him. Neither had anything else. But she suddenly wanted out of the intimate confines of the restaurant and to finish this back on her own turf, where she knew what to do to protect her mind from stray thoughts…and her heart from stray emotions. She decided to go with escape.

"I have a small apartment above the clinic. I can make us a pot of coffee if you want, and we can go over those pictures."

He frowned. "You live in the clinic?"

"Not *in* the clinic, no. Like I said, I have a small studio apartment above it. It saves on transportation costs since I don't have to drive to work."

And it also made it easy to take those middle-of-the-night emergency calls, since all she had to do was throw on some scrubs and walk down a flight of stairs to get to her clinic.

"Were you there when that window was broken?"

No, she'd been in the process of breaking things off with Tyler that night. It had taken her almost three weeks to get the window repaired. Something she wasn't going to tell James, because she had the strange sensation he wouldn't be happy about that. Why he would even care, though, was beyond her.

"I was out that night. But it turned out to be

nothing. No big drama. No one was hiding inside the clinic."

His frown deepened. "You went in by yourself?"

No. Tyler had gone in and checked the place out, even though she could tell he'd been crushed by their breakup. She'd tried to take a taxi home, but he'd insisted on driving her.

He was a good man, a simple man with simple tastes, and Mila wished with all her heart that she could have fallen in love with him. But you couldn't control who you loved. She'd found that out the hard way—had mooned after James, even as she'd flown off to the jungles of Brazil to get away from her pain.

And it had worked. She'd come back a changed person. At least she'd thought she had. Now she wasn't so sure.

"No, I had someone with me."

James swallowed, if that jerky movement of his throat could be called a swallow.

"I'm glad." He called for the check and slipped a credit card into the padded folder. "I'll take you up on that coffee, if the offer is still open. It'll give us a chance to pick a couple of pictures and get them to the marketing department in time for the opening in a few weeks."

As soon as the waiter returned with his receipt, James pocketed it and his card and stood. Mila followed, now wondering if it wouldn't have been better to have their coffee here. She'd wanted to get back to her own territory, but was it really wise to invite the tiger into your sanctuary?

Melodramatic, Mila.

But as she slid into the leather seat of his luxury car, she wondered if she really was being ridiculous. The closer they got to the clinic, the more her nerve endings twitched in dismay. This was a mistake. She knew it was but it was also far too late to change her mind, not without him knowing she was afraid to be alone with him.

They turned onto the road where her clinic was located just as her cell phone sounded with a weird chirp, the one she'd preprogrammed to sound if the silent alarm on her clinic was tripped.

"Oh, no."

Just as James glanced her way, a question in his eyes, she saw her worst fears were realized. The glass door to her clinic had been smashed wide open.

James saw it too, and screeched to a halt just outside the entry. Before either of them could say a word a figure in dark clothing dashed out through the opening and sprinted down the street.

CHAPTER THREE

"STAY HERE!"

James gritted out the command as he threw open the door to his vehicle and dashed after the intruder. He turned the same corner as the man, only to be confronted by a spiderweb of alleys and apartment fronts. There was no sign of anyone. No witnesses. No perpetrator.

If Mila hadn't still been in the car, he would have ventured farther to make sure the jerk wasn't hiding in one of the dumpsters or behind one of the parked cars, but what if he had an accomplice? What if, even now, Mila had decided to go inside her clinic on her own?

"Hell." He should have just called the police and stayed with her, but the instinct to chase down whoever it was had been too strong. And now he was at least five minutes away from the clinic.

Pivoting toward the opening of the alley, he took off the way he'd come, his gaze seeking out his car as soon as he turned the corner. And found the passenger door open, the seat empty.

"Damn it, Mila!"

The muttered words were swallowed by the flow of traffic on the busy street. Why had no one stopped to help when they'd seen someone breaking in? Maybe because this wasn't the safest area of town.

And Mila lived here…had just gone into that dark clinic all alone.

Reaching the door, he found it still locked, so he stepped through the opening, glass crunching beneath his shoes. His instinct was to call out to her, but if someone else was lurking in the shadows, he was afraid he'd tip him off. Instead, he stopped for a second and listened.

He heard someone talking. Was it just Mila on her phone, reporting the break-in to the police? Or was someone else in there?

Picking his footsteps a little more carefully to avoid snapping more glass, he made his way through the inky interior. She hadn't turned the lights on. Why?

He reached the narrow hallway and drew up an internal map of the clinic from his visit a week ago. The voices were coming from the right, from the direction of the exam room he remembered seeing. Pausing outside the open door, he again heard Mila's voice, the low sound coming across as calm and soothing…as if worried about spooking a frightened animal.

It was then that it dawned on him. She wasn't speaking English. It was Spanish. She'd trekked through the Amazon basin, so she knew both Spanish and Portuguese.

He took a deep breath and spun around the corner, a streetlamp shining outside the window making it a little easier to see.

Mila, who was crouching in the gloom, grappling with someone or something, squeaked out a warning. He braced himself for attack.

Only the fear on her face was aimed squarely at him, not whatever was next to her.

"God, James, you almost gave us a heart attack."

He'd almost given *them*…? The thing next to her was evidently a who…not a what.

"What the hell is going on?"

Reaching to the right, where he remembered the light switch being, he flipped it on. Two pairs of eyes blinked up at him. His attention swiveled to the small figure huddled close to Mila.

It was a child—a young boy around three years old—not an armed intruder, like he'd feared. Which meant the man who'd run away from the building was what? A father? Boyfriend? Some kind of sexual predator…? His brows drew together in anger. Who broke into a medical clinic and dropped off a kid?

In one hand, the boy clutched a gray blanket, the satin edge frayed and missing in spots. The child's other hand was balled into a fist that he held against his mouth.

No. Not a fist. The child was sucking his thumb, fingers curled tightly into the palm of his hand. And those hollow, tearstained eyes…

The child stared at him for a second or two longer and then whimpered, cringing closer to Mila. James forced his frown away, realizing he probably made a scary figure standing over them, the emotions churning within him clearly visible.

"Está bien. No tengas miedo." Mila's voice was soft and comforting, even as she sent James another scathing glare.

She was telling the *child* not to be afraid?

What about him? She'd almost set him flat on his ass when he'd seen her kneeling there, envisioning all kinds of terrible things.

But this child was thin. Very thin and… His gaze stopped, chest squeezing tight enough to stop him from breathing for several seconds.

His feet. The boy's feet. They were turned inward at an unnatural angle as if they were pairing up for a duel.

Clubbed. Both of them.

His inward curse rattled his ribs and shunted the pressure that had been gathering around his midsection to his throat. The deformity should have been corrected when the child was an infant.

He knelt next to the pair, his glance meeting Mila's. "Is this one of your patients?"

"No." She placed a hand on the boy's head as if protecting him. From what? James's fury?

He wasn't angry. Not at the child, anyway. "I thought I told you to wait in the car."

"I was going to, but I heard crying coming from inside the clinic." She glanced toward the door just as the sound of a siren swept through the interior of the space. "And I knew the police would arrive at any second."

Not soon enough to stop a bullet, though, if Mila had come upon something other than a frightened child. His anger came back in a rush. "You should have waited for them, then. For your own protection."

Her face quieted, becoming an icy cold mask that stopped him in his tracks. "I don't need you to protect me, and you're not the one who makes my decisions. Not in the past. And certainly not now."

She was right. She was a grown woman, and this was her clinic. Not his. "I was worried. I lost sight of the man I was chasing, and when I came back and saw the car empty…"

Mila's mask cracked, then fell away. "I'm fine." Her head shifted toward the boy. "He said his uncle left him here. I think he was hoping to get the boy some help."

"Medical help, I assume." He nodded toward the boy's feet.

"Yes."

"And then just ran off? What kind of a—?" He bit off the word, not sure how much English the boy understood. "What kind of person does something like that?"

"Fear can make people do things they wouldn't normally do."

"Like abandon someone they're supposed to love?"

As he said the words he was gripped by a huge sense of irony. Fear had caused him to do that very thing. Abandon Mila on the cusp of their wedding, leaving her hurt and alone. No matter that he'd thought it a necessity at the time. And then when he'd discovered it hadn't been necessary, when it had been too late to take it all back, the tabloids had exploded with the news of their broken engagement, comparing it to his parents' ugly divorce years earlier. It had reminded him of all the reasons he should just leave things as they were. Mila deserved better than him and his dysfunctional family.

Freya had been there to pick up the pieces for her friend, and to rake him over the coals. He didn't think his sister had ever quite forgiven him for what he'd done to her dear friend.

The sound of voices shouting from the entrance to the clinic cut off anything she might have been getting ready to say, and they were soon caught up in chaos as the police rushed in, followed by the emergency technicians once the all clear was given.

Worse was the fact that a lone firefighter showed up, right on the heels of everyone else. Concerned eyes took in the scene, and Mila stood to hug him, leaning in to whisper something in his ear.

The man shrugged with a crooked smile. "I know. I was worried. Sorry. The address that came over the com was for Bright Hope. I had to check it out."

Tyler Richardson, Mila's ex. He evidently wasn't out of the picture as completely as Mila had said. And he was evidently allowed to worry about her safety, whereas he himself didn't have that privilege.

Taking in the lean muscle and short cropped hair of the other man, James stiffened. Emotions he'd thought long dead surfaced as he watched her describe what had happened, including the police officers in her explanation.

Mila never once lost her cool during the events that followed, and she didn't allow James—or even her ex—to speak for her, not that the man tried. He knew enough not to, which made James's chest tighten further. Tyler knew the woman Mila was today.

He forced himself to stand a few feet back and watched her, a strange sense of admiration rolling through him. She was confident and matter-of-fact. So different from the shy but passionate woman who had taken his senses by storm six years ago.

She'd traveled the world. Alone. Had probably faced hundreds of situations far more dangerous than the one they'd found at the clinic.

Would she have gotten the chance to grow and change if they'd stayed together? Or would the overprotective nature his sister accused him of having press her into a box she was afraid to leave? Or worse?

He had no idea whether he was trying to assuage his guilt in leaving her, or if it was a genuine question for which there was no answer. But, whatever it was, Mila had been changed in some undefinable way.

The firefighter who still stood by her side seemed to respect her as well. In fact, the three of them—woman, child and man—looked like the kind of family you saw on greeting cards.

And James didn't like it. At all.

He moved in closer to diffuse the picture. "I know Bright Hope hasn't officially opened its branch at The Hills, but I'd like to transport him there to do a workup and make sure there are no medical issues other than his feet. We have state-of-the-art equipment."

It was true. Not just that. His medical center was also equipped with suites to house patients who were having surgery so that their privacy could be guaranteed. A nod to battles he, his sister, and his parents had fought with the paparazzi. The center could also accommodate those patients who needed physical therapy after a procedure. And they always kept a few of the small apartments open for emergencies.

"That would be great. Thank you, James."

Tyler's head abruptly cranked around to look at him, narrowed eyes meeting his.

Was it his imagination or was there a veiled threat in the firefighter's gaze? He met the look and matched it with one of his own. Neither looked away, until Mila cleared her throat and glanced from one to the other.

James took a step back. "I'll call Adam Walker

and see if he has any openings in his schedule. He's one of the best orthopedic surgeons around."

Mila's eyes closed for a second. When they opened, they were a warm shade of hazel that he hadn't seen in forever. "Thank you. I owe you."

"Nope. You don't."

If there was a debt owed by anyone, it was him. And it was more than he could ever begin to repay. For helping him discover something that had set his life path in stone. Or maybe he had Freya, his dad and Cindy to thank for that. Cindy's lie had saved two incompatible people a lot of grief and heartache. Mila might not have appreciated that back when he'd broken things off, but she probably did now.

It took almost an hour to sort through the red tape of having Leonardo—the name the boy had given them—declared a temporary ward of the state so that they could transport him to The Hollywood Hills Clinic. Mila had gone outside to say goodbye to Tyler and then had headed up to her apartment to pack a small overnight bag, insisting that she was going to stay with Leo at the medical center.

What if he got scared? Or had a nightmare? He shouldn't be alone.

"Are you sure you want to stay?"

The department of children's services wouldn't be there until morning. Maybe it was just as well, because James was suddenly bone tired in a way he hadn't been for a long time. Whether it was physical exhaustion or exhaustion that came from the emotional upheaval of the break-in and seeing Mila's ex, he had no idea.

"I'm sure," she said, walking with the EMT workers to the ambulance and then climbing in beside the boy. "Would you mind running by the store and picking up a few things for him, like clothes and a toothbrush?"

"Excuse me?"

"Oh, sorry." She peered out of the vehicle before opening her purse.

He stopped her with an upraised hand, realizing she'd misunderstood him. And he was glad that she'd chosen him to run her errands, rather than Tyler. If he refused, he had no doubt she would call the other man and ask him to get the items. Not going to happen. "I don't need your money. I just have no idea what size he wears."

Up went Mila's brows. "Um. He's around three years old. So a size three should do it. Get some underwear and socks too, okay?"

Kids' clothes sizes ran by age? Who knew?

"I'll meet you back at the clinic in an hour or so."

"Thanks. I'll see you soon."

The doors to the ambulance slammed shut and the vehicle sped away from the building, lights flashing, leaving him standing there alone.

Just as well.

He needed time to untangle exactly what had happened here tonight. And why the fishing hook he'd been toying with a few hours ago at the restaurant had just been suddenly and expertly set by some distant fisherman, leaving him little or no chance of escape. Not without inflicting some major damage to some of his internal organs. Although, if things got too bad, he might have to just rip free of the line and hope for the best.

Adam Walker met her at the door.

Mila tried to calm her still shaking legs. She'd been shocked that Tyler had rushed over to Bright Hope to try to help. Especially with James there.

She'd felt guilty enough for breaking things off with him. She certainly hadn't expected him to show up right after she'd been wined and dined by her other ex.

Lord.

It was over. With both of them. She had nothing to feel guilty about.

And yet she did. That line of guilt ran from her to each man, and she wasn't sure which side made her feel worse.

Neither. And her mind should be on Leo right now, who needed her help.

"Let's get him to an exam room." Adam stretched his palm toward the boy, who, seated in a wheelchair, hesitated for a split second and then placed his small hand in the other man's. With kind eyes and tightly curled brown hair, the orthopedic surgeon had worked with children before. It was there in the easy grip of his fingers, in the way his right shoulder stooped low so Leo's arm wouldn't be stretched too high by the difference in their heights as Mila pushed the wheelchair.

Mila smiled, despite herself. Whereas James had seemed vastly uncomfortable in the boy's presence, Adam was a natural. Judging from the gleaming gold band on the man's left hand, he might even have children of his own at home.

They got Leo up on the exam table, and while a nurse worked on getting the boy's vitals, Adam rolled the bottoms of the child's threadbare jeans up a few inches to get a better look at his feet and ankles.

His jaw tightened as he examined the twisted appendages and slid his gloved hand along the outside edges of Leo's feet. "They're both fixed in the varus position."

Mila knew that there were two main forms of club foot, equinus—when the toes were pointed toward the ground—and varus, when the bone malformation caused the outer portion of the foot to swivel downward, forcing the toes toward the center. "I haven't seen him walk yet. I'm not sure if he can."

"You may not have seen it, but he does." Adam gestured her closer. "See this callusing over the tarsal and metatarsal? He walks on the edges of his feet."

"Wow. It should have been corrected when he was a baby."

Adam shrugged. "I've seen more of these cases

in developing countries than here in the States, where corrective surgery is the norm. Maybe his folks couldn't afford it. Or maybe they immigrated here from somewhere else."

"He only speaks Spanish, from what I've seen. And he said his uncle left him at my clinic. The authorities are still trying to locate him."

The surgeon rubbed a hand behind his neck. "I can fix his feet. But we'll need permission from someone before I can do anything."

"I'm scheduled to speak with a social worker tomorrow. Surely they'll make a way, even if we can't find the uncle. He can't stay like this."

"I've done a few pro bono cases that have come through the courts when the system's doctors were inundated and couldn't get to them." He gave the boy's shoulder a squeeze. "I'll be happy to help in any way I can. Just get me the release forms."

"I'll get to work on it."

James pushed through the door, his arms loaded with packages. Not from the local store but from one of the upper-end clothing chains in the area. The orthopedist's brows went up, bland amusement sliding through his eyes. "Doing a little late-night shopping, James?"

"Sure. That's what I normally do with my free time."

His voice was a little sharper than she'd expected it to be, and she blinked up at him. Maybe he really had minded going to the store. She could have asked Tyler to go, but since they were no longer an item, she hadn't felt right doing so. She didn't want to give him any false hope.

So why had she been okay with asking James? Maybe because she hadn't been worried about him getting the wrong idea. He'd been the one to break off their engagement, not her, so he wasn't likely to want to rekindle anything at this late date.

And neither was she.

Oh, maybe she'd taken one look at that rugged face and piercing blue eyes and had seen stars for a second or two. But that had been pure fantasy. The real-life version of that relationship had gone up in smoke. And if she were stupid enough to harbor any ideas, she'd better snuff them out now because the man hadn't wanted her back then, and he undoubtedly didn't want her now.

Adam filled James in on what surgery to Leo's feet would entail and how long it and the ensuing recovery would take, while Mila peered into the bags of clothes.

Hmm. Superheroes. She never would have pegged James for a superhero kind of guy, although he was aloof and secretive. And he never snatched at publicity. In fact, he'd always shunned it while they'd been together, even though reporters had dogged his every step back then.

Was it because he hadn't wanted to be seen with her?

He'd asked her to marry him, for heaven's sake.

And yet he hadn't been able to go through with it in the end. How humiliating it had been to see cringe-worthy pictures of herself beneath headlines that had screamed things like "scorned" and "dumped." She'd fled to Brazil to get away from the onslaught...and the pain.

Pulling her mind from the past, she ripped open the packages, instead. "I wish we could run these through the washer before putting them on him, but I guess it's better than staying in the filthy things he has on now. I'd like to get him to a room and get him cleaned up, if we can."

James pulled his cell phone from his pocket and made a quick call. "Okay, mark the suite as occupied. Oh, and, Stella, make sure you have an extra trundle bed set up."

Good, he was taking her at her word that she wanted to stay in the room with Leo.

"Yes, I'm aware that the room already has one. I need an extra, in case there are any problems."

"Problems?" The panicked word slid from her mouth before she could stop it.

Adam, as if sensing a storm was brewing, gave a quick wave. "Let me know what happens with the social worker, or if there's a problem during the night. I'm on call."

She mouthed, "Thank you," to him, still trying to wrap her head around the bombshell James had just dropped. Why on earth did he need an extra bed? Did he think she couldn't handle one small child on her own?

As soon as the specialist was out of the room, she turned toward him. "I don't understand."

"You don't know this child or what he's like. It's just for one night, to make sure things run smoothly."

Smoothly? He was making Leo sound like he was just another chart to be dealt with.

As if realizing he needed to clarify matters,

he said, "If it's true that his uncle dropped him off, the boy is bound to be frightened. He might even try to run away or the uncle could show up, which could cause legal problems for the clinic if the Department of Children and Family Services comes by tomorrow and the child has disappeared. I thought we could take shifts and watch him. See how he does."

Okay, so that made sense. Although she wasn't sure how he expected a three-year-old to sneak down the hallways unnoticed and make a daring escape. But he could get lost. Or hurt. Or someone could appear, claiming to be one of his parents.

At least James's reasons for staying with them were now perfectly clear. It had everything to do with protecting the reputation of his precious medical center.

And nothing to do with her.

She heard something.

Cracking her eyelids, Mila found a dark, silent room.

Not her bedroom.

Lying there for a moment, she waited for her vision to adjust.

Another murmur of sound.

Leo! She was in a hospital suite. Rolling to the side, she almost tumbled off the narrow cot until the events of the previous evening came flooding back to her. The boy. His damaged feet. James's insistence on spending the night with them.

She somehow managed to get her legs beneath her and staggered upright as a quiet sniffle and whisper slid past her.

Yanking down the T-shirt she'd retrieved from her apartment, she tiptoed toward the sounds, hoping she could get there before Leo woke up James. If she could do that and leave the lights off, she would.

More snuffling, and then a deep sigh.

She could finally see enough to make out the cot where James had been.

It was empty.

She relaxed. Maybe he'd decided not to stay after all. If he'd had as difficult a time getting to sleep as she had…

Well, *her* stupid insomnia was due to having James sleeping in the same room.

She made her way toward the hospital bed, almost reaching it before she realized there were two figures there.

Her heart squeezed so tight she almost couldn't breathe. There in the bed was James, eyes closed, one arm loosely draped around Leo, keeping him from falling off the edge. The boy, dressed in the new set of superhero pajamas, was half-sprawled across her ex's chest. Tears pricked her eyes.

Their future could have looked exactly like this, only she would have been in the bed beside James, and Leo would have been their son.

She had to blink several times to get the chaos swirling within her to settle down enough to move closer. Leo must have woken sometime during the night. James had evidently heard him and she hadn't and he had gone to him.

Since it looked like one of Leo's hands was clutching James's shirt, rather than his ratty blanket, he probably couldn't ease away from him.

How long had they been here like this?

From James's posture, it had been a while. His right arm was curled beneath his head, as if using it for a pillow, since the actual pillow was on the boy's side of the bed. Except Leo wasn't using it. He was using James's chest instead.

She crept closer, fascinated, just as she'd always been, by how her ex's face looked as he slept. His lashes made slight shadows beneath his eyes. The furrow of concentration he normally had between his brows was softened in sleep, and just the slightest hint of a depression remained.

She should go back to bed and leave them alone, but she couldn't. It wasn't fair to let him shoulder the burden when she had been the one to insist on staying with him in the room.

So she leaned down, close to his ear. "James," she whispered.

His lids flicked open in an instant, all traces of sleep gone. Blue eyes sought out hers and the arm holding Leo to him tightened slightly.

The frown was back. "You okay?"

"Yes." She nodded to the sleeping boy. "Did he wake up?"

"He had a nightmare."

There was something about whispering with James in the dark that made her swallow. How easy things had once been between them, and how simple they'd seemed.

In reality, nothing had been simple. They'd known each other for too short a period of time to commit to staying with each other forever. She'd known almost nothing about him and yet she'd planned on spending the rest of her life with him.

An ocean of hurt welled up inside her, making its way to her eyes once again.

James didn't miss it. Then again, he didn't miss much of anything. His arm came from beneath his head and he snagged her wrist. "Hey. Are you sure you're okay?"

"Yes." Her voice betrayed her, though, even at a whisper.

"Mi." He eased out of the bed, leaving Leo asleep, and his hand moved from her wrist to the hair falling over the left side of her face, coaxing it behind her ear. The soft touch made her shudder. Before she could move away, though, his fingers continued from her ear, curling around until they reached her nape. He paused.

Then his head came down, lips brushing against hers in a soft kiss that broke her heart.

"I'm sorry," he murmured. "For everything."

Sorry.

An admission of guilt but nothing else.

A word rolled through her, bouncing around like a giant ball that had been trapped in a small room for far too long. There was no exit unless she made one. But, try as she might, her pride wouldn't allow her to ask the one question that had haunted her for six long years: why?

CHAPTER FOUR

JAMES FELT AS if he'd been kicked in the skull by a donkey.

Exhausted, and with a pounding head to boot, he'd been forced to take a couple of painkillers. Something that went against the grain, after dealing with his mother's addiction problems. Problems that had probably contributed to Freya's own addiction to controlling her food. Thankfully, his sister had overcome those issues and was now leading a happy, healthy life.

He paused outside the door to the exam room, bracing himself for his "emergency" patient, Peggy Smith, better known as Patricia Stillwell, award-winning actress. It was always an emergency, it seemed, whenever she stepped into his office. With raven hair and thick dark lashes, she'd been compared to Elizabeth Taylor on several occasions.

She also won the award for being his most difficult patient, obsessed with maintaining an age-less appearance that was not realistic. He'd talked her out of many a procedure, using a computer manipulation program that showed her what the results would be. And when putting up before and after images didn't work, he then resorted to showing her what she would look like ten years down the road. So far it had worked, but he knew the day was coming when she would no longer be willing to listen and would start demanding he comply. When that day came, he would refer her to another doctor.

He was pretty sure she wouldn't go quietly but would trumpet some ugly rumor about him to the tabloids to make him pay. She'd done it with her primary care physician when he'd refused to pre-scribe her a heftier dose of sleep aids. That doctor had wound up in the divorce courts by the time Patricia had finished with him.

It was just as well that he had nothing to destroy as far as romantic ties went.

He pushed open the door without bothering to look at the chart. The sight that greeted him, how-ever, was not Patricia Stillwell, petulant actress.

It was the tearful, scrubbed-clean face of a terrified woman.

Holding a bloody towel up to her cheek, she looked devastated. And slightly out of it.

James did flip open the chart at this unexpected turn of events. "What happened?"

"I…slipped…in the shower." Patricia's voice was uneven. Not slurred, exactly, but there was an odd tremor to it. "Cut my cheek a little."

He punched the button for the nurse. Unlike what he would have expected from the actress, she didn't once mention her appearance or ask about scarring. That made him even more uneasy.

"Who brought you in?" He'd seen no one waiting in the hallway, not even her current love interest who was also an A-list actor.

"Allen." Patricia wouldn't quite meet his gaze. "But he had a casting call and had to drop me off at the back entrance to the clinic."

Another warning flag began fluttering in his head. Allen Claremont had a reputation for losing his temper both on the set and with his fans and paparazzi. He'd been arrested on assault charges on a couple of occasions, but the charges had always been dropped. "Let's take a look."

When the towel came down, James caught his breath. This was no "little cut." Neither was it the jagged split he would have expected from a hard fall, but a clean, straight, slice that ran from the corner of her mouth up the side of her cheek. Blood immediately gathered along the wound. He swore under his breath and grabbed a sterile gauze dressing, ripping it open and pressing it to the injury to slow the bleeding.

He didn't hold back the question, didn't even consider doing so. "Did Allen do this?"

"No! Of course not! If the press even suspects, it'll ruin him."

The answer had come much too quickly. As if she'd been rehearsing the words. The nurse came in before he could ask anything else, and Patricia's shoulders slumped.

"I'll need to flush it and test your nerve function." He hesitated to go any further, but she needed to know that this wasn't something that he could wave a magic wand over. "This is a serious injury. The placement makes hiding it more difficult. And if there are nerves involved, we'll need to call in Damien Moore, our head of reconstructive surgery."

"I'll be able to go back to work, though."

That strange slur was still there. The arm holding the cloth to her cheek had obscured some of her mouth movements, but James was worried. There was an abundance of nerves and vessels in the cheek. If the cut was deep enough, it could affect muscle function.

"Of course you will."

But at forty-five, she'd already complained that the quality of the roles she was being offered had declined. This injury could be life-altering for her.

Allen, in his thirties, was almost a decade younger than Patricia. He was a sought-after actor in romantic comedies, for sure, but he was still climbing the ladder. There was talk that he was using Patricia's success as a way to boost his own, using her contacts and prestige to cement his position. If what he suspected was true, though, Patricia needed to report him.

But would she?

"I need to leave without the paparazzi wondering why I came here."

The clinic valued the privacy of its patients because James insisted on it. With that in mind, one of the first things to go in had been an enclosed entrance where drivers could pull up and drop off occupants and then slide back out without anyone being able to see, thanks to a stone wall that faced the street. The result was a blind spot where it was virtually impossible for photographers—or anyone else—to spy on the comings and goings of patients.

That reminded him. He'd won a small victory this past week with the board of directors. He'd convinced them that Bright Hope should have an entrance inside the main part of the clinic. The argument that those patients had as much right to privacy as The Hollywood Hills Clinic's own patients did had evidently held water. They'd scrapped the plans to permanently close the door that connected the two wings. The clinics would now be linked in every sense of the word.

"That won't happen for a while. We need to clean out the wound and check for damage to the structure of your face."

"Can't you put some of your famous tiny stitches in and make it go away?"

This wasn't going away. Not completely. It would leave a scar. Maybe it wouldn't be noticeable to the cameras of the paparazzi but it would be there nonetheless.

Kind of like the scar he carried around? It wasn't an external scar but he still felt the pull inside him when his heart got too involved with a patient. That warning tug that told him to take a few steps back.

"Stitches, yes. But we're going to have to do it under anesthesia. It'll take a couple of hours, and I'd feel better if you stayed overnight."

Her eyes widened. "But Allen—"

"Will be fine. And if you're lying to me about his part in this, then you need to wise up and put some distance between you. Do you want him doing this to someone else?"

"He won't. I know he won't."

That was the closest to an admission he was going to get. "How do you know?"

She shrugged an overly thin shoulder. "I just do."

Because he'd told her he was sorry? That he'd never do it again? He could remember his father promising the same thing to his mother after each infidelity.

Maybe Allen—unlike Michael Rothsberg—

meant it. After all James meant it when he said he wasn't having children. And so far he'd kept that promise. But life was full of unknowns. He hadn't expected Cindy to claim she was pregnant and force him into a decision he'd never expected to make.

He sighed and shook his head. "I want you to think about something while I set up for surgery. If that cut had been three inches lower, we might not be talking about restorative surgery. We'd be fighting to save your life. Next time you might not be so lucky."

James took that "next time" philosophy to heart in his own life. He always, always used protection, no matter how insistent his current partner was that she was clean and on birth control. You never knew what someone was capable of.

Like Cindy.

Or his father.

The bastard.

Evidently Patricia was opting to learn about personal failings the hard way. As difficult as she was as a patient, he didn't like knowing someone had purposely tried to destroy her life. And for an actress, a maiming slash to the face was to strike at the heart of how she made a living.

But who knew what went on in the heads of some of these celebrities? He certainly didn't claim to know his famous parents, whose public meltdowns had probably kept half the tabloids in America in business. His mom's repeated stints in rehab had probably done the same for the other half. He barely had contact with them anymore.

"Think about it," he urged.

Patricia's chin wobbled, and her hand went up to the gauze pad covering her damaged cheek. "I will."

A muscle contracted in James's jaw. "What do you want us to do if he comes to visit?"

"I don't know." Her eyes closed for a second. "Can I decide that after I wake up from surgery?"

"Yes." It was the best he was going to get for the moment. "I'll put a no-visitors order on your chart." Which he did even as he spoke, pushing a button on his tablet and checking the appropriate box on Patricia's chart, quickly typing what he wanted done and when. The tablets were connected to a central system that would flag the next available surgical suite and reserve it, along with his team. Then he called Damien and asked if he could come in and give him a second opinion.

The other surgeon promised he could be there in twenty minutes.

While he waited, he gave Patricia a local injection of lidocaine with epinephrine to numb the wound and slow bleeding and flushed the area with saline, examining the edges of the laceration with his magnifying headset. Thank God, she wasn't dealing with full tissue laceration as the wound didn't penetrate the mucosal or muscle tissue, but it was deep enough that he would have to do the repairs in layers. He mentally calculated fifty stitches on the surface and absorbable suture material inside the wound.

He noticed that as she'd talked, that slight defect in her speech had cleared up. Maybe it had been caused by stress, rather than nerve damage.

A knock on the door pulled him from his work and he sat up, tipping the loupes to the top of his head. He glanced at his tablet. Maybe one of the surgical suites had come available sooner than they'd expected.

Nope. The projections still put them at an hour out. Luckily the face had an overabundance of blood vessels, so there was a longer window for repairs than for some other areas of the body, where the lack of blood supply created a need for quick intervention.

He glanced at the nurse. "Can you stay with her for a minute?"

Patricia grabbed his hand. "You're not leaving me, are you?"

His heart went icy. Those were almost exactly the same words Mila had used on the last night they had been intimate. He'd gotten out of bed almost immediately, guilt eating him alive. She'd known something had been wrong and had tried to get him to talk.

You're not leaving me, are you?

He'd denied it at the time, even as he'd known he was indeed going to leave her. He'd fallen into bed with her in despair, days after Cindy had told him he was going to be a father. He'd meant to talk, not have sex, but once the deed had been done, it had been easier to play the denial game than to have it out with her. Then it had been too late. He'd broken things off just as he'd learned that the tabloids were going to break a story about how he and Cindy had been seen together at a hotel days earlier—when she'd told him she was pregnant.

And then his father had...

Not the time, James.

This wasn't about him. It was about Patricia. "I'm not leaving. I'll be right back."

When he opened the door he swallowed hard.

The woman he'd just been thinking about was standing there, worry in her hazel eyes. "What is it? Leo?"

He stepped into the hall and closed the door behind him.

She nodded. "They think his uncle has fled to Mexico. All they found at his apartment was a note saying the boy's parents had been killed by one of the drug cartels and that he wanted a better life for Leo than what he could get in his home country."

Her face was as white as a sheet. Mila had told him her parents had been murdered when she'd been a child and that her aunt had lied to her for years about how they'd died. Was she remembering that?

Gripping her hand in his, he lowered his voice. "I'm so sorry, Mi. Are you okay?"

"What am I going to tell him?"

"Nothing, for now. He's only three years old." He took a step closer. "If you're thinking about your parents, this isn't the same thing. You were older and your aunt *never* told you the truth, and she should have. Just not when you were Leo's age."

"Maybe. But after a while it becomes easier to let the lie stand than to have the courage to do what needs to be done. I don't want his trust destroyed like mine was."

A shot of hot bile stormed James's throat. He'd done exactly that with Mila. Destroyed her trust. And, yes, it had been far too easy to let the lie stand. Even now.

"Was his uncle abandoning him a better choice? I don't think so."

Hell. Why did every word out of his mouth seethe with accusation? But not at the wayward uncle. At James. At what he'd done six years ago.

He'd wanted Mila to have a better life than what he could give her. To do that, he'd done much the same thing as Leo's uncle had. And Mila's aunt. He'd lied to protect her.

From the angry flash of her eyes he wondered

if she knew what he'd done six years ago. If so, there was no plastic surgery known to man that could repair that particular scar. It was far too old and covered too great an area. He'd thought cutting things off with her would leave a clean line… an easy fix.

How wrong he'd been.

He opted to change the subject. "What did DCFS say?"

"That as long as he's in the hospital they can hold off on putting him into foster care, but the second we release him…"

"Will he be deported?"

"If they can find the uncle? Almost certainly." She licked her lips. "I'm thinking about applying to be a foster parent."

"What?" Of all the impulsive, ridiculous things… But that was Mila. Putting others ahead of herself. Always. That had included him once upon a time. "You need to think this through. You're just getting ready to open a clinic here. How are you going to have time to take on something like a child?"

She blinked up at him. "Some*thing*? I don't know. It just feels like the right thing to do."

"You don't even know this child."

"No. But I've known children like him. And maybe this is my chance to change a life. To really, truly—radically—change the future for this boy." Her chest rose. "His parents were killed. Murdered. And he doesn't have an aunt to see that he gets the care he needs, like I did. She loved me, James. No matter how much I disagree with what she did in the end, I know she was trying to keep me from being hurt."

A host of emotions crawled along his nerve endings, none of them good. "Why are you telling me this?"

"Because…" she licked her lips "…I want to use you as a personal reference on the paperwork, if that's okay."

Mila's head swirled as she waited for his answer. She wasn't sure why it was important for James's name to be on that form. Avery would certainly agree to be a reference. But she wanted James. Did she still need his approval somehow?

No. It was strictly a tactic to show she surrounded herself with respected professionals. People with money, although that went against everything she believed in. But since she was asking DCFS to expedite the process, she would use any tactic she could think of.

What she'd told James was the truth. Now that she was back in the States, she still wanted to make a difference. Bright Hope was one thing, but bringing hope to a child who was an orphan like herself, who had nothing…no one…suddenly seemed vital. Maybe she was trying to make sure Leo didn't feel the way she had when her parents had died, leaving her with no living relative other than her aunt. Or the way she'd felt when James had walked away from their relationship, making her feel just as alone as she'd felt after the death of her parents.

"Why me?" His low voice rumbled past her ear and she couldn't tell if he was angry or just puzzled by her request.

Mila wasn't sure she even knew why herself.

"Because you started The Hollywood Hills Clinic. You've worked with DCFS cases before."

"Only a few times. And that was years ago." He frowned. "How did you even know about those?"

"Adam Walker said the clinic has helped DCFS out in the past. And Freya said *you* used to take some of the harder reconstruction cases that no one else wanted."

"Ah, yes. My sister. I should have known."

This was a mistake. A stupid, impulsive mistake. The prospect of working so closely with someone who'd once broken her heart must have addled her thinking somehow. Time to undo it, if she could. Starting with…

"Never mind. I needed a professional reference, but there are plenty of other people I've worked with that I can ask."

He leaned back against the wall and regarded her through hooded eyes. "Like Tyler Richardson?"

She'd actually been thinking of Avery, but what if she did ask Tyler? What was it to James? Something made her pursue that line of thinking. "I'm sure Tyler would be happy to provide me with a reference."

"I'm sure he would." He sighed. "I didn't say I wouldn't give you the reference. I was just surprised you would want it."

"Whatever gives me an edge." Even as she repeated those words inside her head she knew they weren't strictly true.

"I guess I should be flattered, then." He gave her a slow smile. "Yes. You can use my name. I'm sure you've used it before, although not in quite as positive a way."

She smiled back. "No. Probably not." She remembered biting out his name in anger on more than one occasion, usually accompanied by a black period of name-calling and plastic-plate throwing—something her therapist had suggested after she'd found out the truth about her parents' deaths. She still threw around nonbreakable dishware from time to time. Not over James, but just when various frustrations crossed her path. Although if she got Leo, she would have to stop that.

It would be a small price to pay.

She drew a relieved breath. "Well, thank you. I'll get you the paperwork—"

"You haven't heard my conditions yet."

The air in her lungs stuck for a second before whistling back out. "Conditions?"

"I have a cottage on my property. I want you and Leo to live there until you find something else."

"What?" Shock held her immobile for several horrifying seconds. Stay on his property? There was no way.

"Do you really think DCFS is going to let you keep a child on a property that has been broken into on two separate occasions?" His words said one thing, but his eyes said something else, dark shadows preventing her from seeing below the surface.

"But the broken door was Leo's uncle. The window was probably his handiwork as well."

"You don't know that. And unless you can convince them there is no risk to Leo…"

She couldn't. In fact, both incidents had left her shaken. But what else could she do?

It wasn't like she could just up and move to Hollywood Hills. There was no way she could afford to live in this part of the city, even with the increase in her salary. Besides, her tendency was to keep just enough to live on and sock the rest of it away with the small remainder of her inheritance, ready to sink into whatever needy cause caught her attention.

And taking Leo in? Didn't that top the list of good causes?

What about finding James with the boy sprawled across his chest last night? Oh, that had touched her deeply. So deeply that she wanted him to approve of what she was choosing to do? Possibly.

But live within a few yards of his house? As icy and detached as James liked to appear to those around him, he cared. Why else would he agree to be a reference…or insist that she move him onto his property? Did she want to dig any deeper than that? No. She needed to be grateful and leave the explanations for another time.

"Thank you. I accept your condition."

"Good. The place is furnished, but I'll send someone for anything you want to put in there this afternoon."

"It's not permanent. As long as you have the basics, I'll just bring a couple of suitcases of clothes. And once I find a better solution I'll be moving out."

His brows came together but he didn't argue.

She rushed ahead to finish. "I know you have a patient waiting, so I'll let you get back to it. I'm sure DCFS will be calling you with some routine questions. I would appreciate it, though, if you didn't mention our past."

His mouth quirked, and he took a step closer, edging dangerously close to her personal space.

"Do you think they won't find out about us, Mila?" His voice, low and silky, brushed across nerve endings she hadn't even known existed. "All they have to do is type your name into a search engine and mine comes up as well. I've done it, and there are still plenty of pictures of us out there, courtesy of the paparazzi."

Her tummy went wobbly, as did her legs. Only there was nowhere for her to retreat, except to turn and run back down the hall.

How did he know there were pictures of them? He said he'd typed her name in? Why? And what exactly had come up when he had? Six years was a long time for stuff to hang around. But when you had famous parents, as they both did, it stood to reason that people would be interested.

"I'm sure they can find anything, if they look hard enough. I have nothing to hide. But if you could avoid giving them a reason to dig any deeper, I would appreciate it."

He reached out and touched her cheek, and the wobbling became a full-fledged tremor. "Afraid of your skeletons, Mila?"

The correct response came to her in a flash of self-preservation. "No, I'm afraid of yours."

There were probably pictures of him with every starlet or model he'd ever dated. She didn't know if that would hurt her chances or not, but she didn't want to risk it.

His hand fell back to his side, and his eyes cooled back to their normal color. "Don't worry, those particular skeletons will remain safely out of sight."

"Thank you." She hesitated. "For everything."

Just as she started to turn away James touched her arm. "For what it's worth, Mi, you'll make a great mother."

Another doctor came striding down the hallway headed straight for them. James greeted him with a wave and together they went into the exam room, leaving Mila standing there to digest the shocking developments, not only about his cottage but his statement about her being a good mother. Did he really believe that?

She had no idea, but if she was smart she'd forget he'd ever mentioned that.

The question was, was she smart? Where James was concerned? Absolutely not. Sighing, she decided to head down the hallway and look to see how the newest branch of Bright Hope was coming along.

She made several turns down the corridors, catching sight of a couple of people she thought she recognized from the celebrity magazines, but she knew enough not to stare or stop to get a closer look. Then she found a glass door inscribed with the same logo she had on the LA clinic.

Bright Hope.

She'd looked at the plans, and James had told her about the board's decision to allow access through the main part of the medical center, but the reality of seeing it made her heart swell. Soon there would be patients here and a bustling staff. They could reach so many people.

Moving closer, she ran her fingers over the paint. It reminded her that James wanted her to paint a mural on the wall in the reception area similar to the one at her other location.

It was official. In a few short weeks they would open their doors. Which meant she needed to get busy and hire some staff besides Avery. Unless James planned on pulling them from his current pool. Except she wanted to do the hiring herself, to make sure that the clinic personnel wouldn't act put off if someone came in looking a little less than perfect. Surely James would understand that.

She went to push open the door, only to find it locked, which made sense.

Peering through the glass, she smiled when she spotted comfortable-looking furniture in pale, muted colors, rather than the modern black and chrome found in most areas of The Hollywood Hills Clinic.

Maybe she could do the mural over…

A huge framed picture on the wall opposite where she stood caught her eye. She stared, her breath getting stuck in her throat for several long seconds.

Damn. It was a framed enlargement of one of the photos taken at the LA location that James had shown her over dinner. With everything that had happened with Leo, they'd never had a chance to go through them again.

In this particular shot, James had hold of her hand and they were gazing into each other's eyes.

To someone who hadn't been there, it appeared the normal handshake of two businesspeople. But she had been there, and that touch had been no ordinary clasp and release. No, it had been as intimate as his touch in the hallway a few moments earlier. She quickly averted her eyes to glance at the words that appeared under the picture frame.

In beautiful script appeared the words:

The Hollywood Hills Clinic and Bright Hope Two powerful beacons serving our patients and our community.

That was when she knew the picture was there to stay. No matter what she said, the board of directors or whoever had chosen that particular photo had made the decision.

For as long as the two clinics collaborated, there would be handshakes and meetings and unexpected sightings. But there would be no more kisses. Not like the one in Leo's hospital suite.

Moving onto his property where she would see him almost every day would make that a challenge. For her, at least.

But somehow she either needed to become immune to his presence or risk facing some devastating consequences. If she couldn't, then she needed to find someplace else to live as soon as she could. And then have as little as possible to do with this clinic. And with him.

CHAPTER FIVE

THE SOCIAL WORKER was due at his house at any moment, and James still had no idea how things had gotten so screwed up. One second he'd been telling Mila he would be her reference and the next he'd been demanding she use the guest cottage behind his own home.

The thought of her staying above that shabby clinic downtown made his gut churn. It wasn't safe. Not only for Leo but for Mila as well. And since she only had a security guard during the day…

It was a wonder she hadn't been hurt or killed.

Besides, no one stayed in the cottage. He'd purchased the property right after he and Mila had gotten engaged, with the intention that he would use the extra residence for either of his parents, should they choose to visit. Only he and Mila had never made it down the aisle, and he'd never invited his folks to come and visit. In reality, his father wasn't welcome in his home. And his mom, probably unaware of what Michael Rothsberg had tried to do all those years ago, hadn't even asked.

But that didn't mean he should immediately offer the place to Mila to help her become a foster parent. In fact, the thought of having a child on the premises twenty-four-seven made him shudder. And yet he'd done it anyway. And Mila had accepted his offer, which had been another surprise.

It had been a little over a week since she'd turned in the paperwork—a little over a week since he'd been foolish enough to press his lips to hers in Leo's room, although he could still remember every second of it. It seemed the DCFS had indeed expedited things.

The problem had been that Leo couldn't stay at the clinic indefinitely, and once he left, he would be dumped into the foster-care system, which brought up a whole new series of complications. One of them being that The Hollywood Hills Clinic wasn't included on the list of medical facilities that DCFS normally used. So if any of their normal doctors were available, the agency would use them, leaving Adam Walker—and Leo—out in the cold.

And Mila wanted to make sure the boy received the best care. She was willing to become a foster mom and live right under James's nose, if need be, to make that happen.

Mila was at the cottage right now, setting up things in the spare bedroom. She'd stuck with her decision about bringing nothing more than a couple of suitcases. And she'd tried to pay him rent.

Rent!

There was no way in hell he was accepting a dime from Mila. It wasn't a permanent arrangement, and Mila was already looking for a place that allowed children. Which was ridiculous. The child wasn't a puppy. Or a pet. He was a human being.

Something he'd been far too conscious of as he'd held the boy that first night at the clinic. It was the only night James had stayed with them because having a small trusting body curled against him had done a number on his gut. Worse, he'd fallen asleep, and when he'd woken up, Mila had been standing over them with a softness to her eyes that he hadn't seen in a very long time.

He didn't want her getting any strange ideas. Not that she would. There was no way she would ever take him back after what he'd done to her all those years ago. And he wouldn't dream of trying to persuade her otherwise.

And yet he'd been willing to persuade her to live—and sleep—within a hundred yards of his house.

As if sensing he was thinking about her, Mila peered around his open back door. "She just texted me. She's running about a half hour late."

There was something telling about the fact that Mila had come over in person to let him know, rather than simply shooting him a text like the social worker had done with her. It just confirmed the days of sending lighthearted messages back and forth were long gone.

Mila evidently texted some people, though, whereas James chose not to send messages at all. Everyone around him knew about his weird predilection, including his sister, although she just chose to ignore it.

"I'm making coffee," he said. "Would you like a cup?"

"Love one. I have to tell you, I'm nervous. What if she doesn't like me?"

Since James had never met anyone who didn't like Mila, he couldn't imagine that happening. "She will."

"You don't know that." She perched on one of the tall leather chairs that flanked the round bar table and propped an elbow on the black marble surface.

He hesitated. "Are you sure you want to do this, Mila? It could be a long-term commitment."

"Maybe that's what I need. A long-term commitment." She studied her nails, not meeting his eyes.

His gut twisted. It was the one thing she'd needed from him, and the one thing he hadn't been able to give her. "Are you thinking of adopting him?"

"I'll cross that bridge when I come to it. It depends on what happens with his uncle and whether they can locate him."

He poured a mug of coffee, adding flavored creamer and a squirt of whipped cream he had in his fridge. He topped it off with a sprinkle of cinnamon.

When he carried it back to her, she was staring at him strangely.

"What?" he asked.

"You remembered."

He glanced down at the cup, realizing he'd automatically fixed the brew the way he had in the past. The exact way that Mila had drunk it back then.

Setting it in front of her, he swallowed. "I remember a lot of things."

"Like the way I drink my coffee." Her words came out in a husky rush, her tongue tipping forward to moisten her upper lip.

He remembered that gesture too. It had normally ended with him kissing her—with them falling into bed.

"Among other things." Like the way she tasted. Felt beneath his hands. His mouth. A sense of hot anticipation began to roll through him.

The chair was tall enough that it wouldn't take much to lean down and…

She picked up her cup and took a quick sip, then set it down again. He should move away and fix his own cup before he did something stupid.

Really stupid.

Too late.

He slid his fingers into the thick hair at her nape, the delicate bones of her skull also something he remembered far too well.

"James?" The inflection at the end of his name said it was technically a question, but the soft sigh put it in a different category altogether.

Cupping her face, he met her halfway, his lips brushing over hers, his eyes closing as bitter-sweet memories—more sweet than bitter—swept him away on a cloud of forgetfulness.

Forgetting the pain he'd caused her.

Forgetting the horror of Cindy's fake pregnancy.

Forgetting the fury caused by his father's attempt to buy her off.

All that remained was the woman sitting at *his* table in *his* kitchen in *his* house. And he'd forgotten nothing about her. Especially not the needy press of her mouth on his or how it made him want things he'd never dreamed he could have.

One of her hands came up and wound around his neck, her fingers warm from where she'd held the cup of coffee. A feeling so familiar it sent a ripple through the muscles of his abdomen, the sensation pooling in his groin.

This was right where he wanted to be.

He slid his thumbs beneath her chin and tipped her head just a touch, taking a step closer, until his thighs pressed against the outside of her leg.

How easy it would be just to swing her up in his arms and head toward his bedroom. The room where they'd made love time and time again.

Bzzz... Bzzz... Bzzz...

Something vibrated on the table and a flash of movement caught his eye.

Damn! Mila's phone.

She jerked away and grabbed the instrument just before it slid off the table.

The past came rushing back to greet him. All the regrets. All the mistakes.

Mistakes he'd vowed never to repeat.

She pulled her phone toward her, glancing at the screen. She didn't say anything for a second or two, then murmured, "The social worker. She'll be here in five."

Even he could hear the tremor to her voice. And her lips were pink and lush and full. From his kiss. Another thing he hadn't seen in ages. All he wanted to do was lean down and take them again.

But the last thing either of them needed was for someone to jump to the wrong conclusions.

Ha! What kind of conclusions would they be? That they'd been on their way to devouring each other?

"Why don't you run to the restroom, and I'll wait for her."

"Thank you."

With that, Mila slid off the chair and headed down the hallway to where she already knew the restroom was. Which was good. Because it also gave him a chance to try to collect his thoughts. Not that there were many of them floating around his head at the moment. Just a jumble of emotions that he needed to shove to the back of his mind.

Mila was back in two minutes. Much sooner than he'd expected. Her hair gleamed around her face, and those pink, natural lips had a coating of artificial color slicked on, hiding any trace of what had happened. Even her hazel eyes seemed cooler. Much different than the warm ocean green they'd been just before he'd kissed her.

He smiled, half in relief and half in regret. "You look poised and ready."

How easy it had been for her to wipe away any

trace of what had happened. Had it been just as easy for her to erase what they'd once meant to each other? He had spent many sleepless nights thinking about her.

If only there'd been a lip balm back then that could have erased the memories of her mouth opening beneath his. Of sinking deep into her and losing his heart, his soul…his mind.

This was not helping.

"Do you want to meet her here or at the cottage?"

"The cottage, since that's where we'll be staying. At least in the beginning. Thank you again for suggesting it. And you were right. My apartment wouldn't have worked. I would have worried constantly about Leo. Especially after what happened."

Thinking back, James was pretty sure the first broken window was related to the boy and his uncle as well. But she had a point. There'd been a police report filed about the first incident. And the second. That wouldn't have played in Mila's favor during the home visit.

"Speaking of which, I had a lease agreement drawn up. I should have mentioned it earlier, but it's just a technicality. Just in case the social worker wants something official."

And to make it look less like a friends with benefits arrangement. Because they weren't friends. Not anymore. And there were definitely no benefits attached.

"I never even thought of that. Thank you. I'll pay rent, of course."

"I already told you that isn't necessary. It was just sitting empty, anyway. My housekeeper did her best to keep the place clean but—"

"It was spotless. And I won't need her to clean for me. I'm a big girl, I can take care of myself."

"And I'm a grown man, but we both have very demanding schedules, and yours is about to get a whole lot busier with the opening of the new clinic."

In fact, it had been James's mother who had hired his housekeeper years ago. He'd protested at first, but when he'd seen how Rosa's face had fallen when he had tried to let her down as easily as he could, he'd had second thoughts. He'd justified it the same way he'd justified it to Mila, telling himself he was busy and it wouldn't hurt to have a little help on the side.

But a big part of it was that he couldn't bear to let one more woman down, as if by keeping Rosa employed he was paying just a little bit of penance for letting Mila down. For letting his mom down by not telling her what his father had done. So Rosa was there to stay.

"Still—"

"You'll hurt her feelings if you try to refuse her help. Besides, she loves children. I think it would be a plus in your favor if the social worker knew you'd have someone to watch Leo when you weren't home."

"I don't expect Rosa to do that without asking her first."

His housekeeper was off on Fridays so that she could spend weekends with her nephews who lived in Fresno. Since she stayed on the premises the rest of the week, it also gave James a few days of privacy when he could unwind. Or pass the time in female company.

Come to think of it, it had been a while since he'd spent time with a woman. Maybe that's what was behind his sudden urge to kiss Mila. He needed to have sex.

With anyone *but* Mila.

The doorbell rang just as he was trying to convince himself of that. That any woman would do.

Except there was a little voice deep inside that rumbled that that was a lie. There was only one woman who would do, and she was the very one he couldn't have. The very one he shouldn't touch.

Not anymore.

James could charm the pants off a giraffe.

The social worker had been hooked from the moment she'd laid eyes on him, flipping her fake blond hair over her shoulder every other second.

Good thing the woman had arrived when she had, though, because James had almost charmed the pants off her as well.

The last thing she needed was to fall back under his spell. Hadn't she learned her lesson the first time?

Evidently not because she was practically living under his roof. In fact, that damned lease—the one she'd scribbled her name on just before they'd opened the door to the social worker—said she had free rein, not only of the cottage but also the main house. She could come and go as she pleased. Use the pool, or anything else that she wanted.

Including him?

No. Not including him. And she would not set foot in the main house any more than absolutely necessary. She would take him up on his offer of the pool, though, because she imagined that swimming would be a great low-impact therapy for Leo as he recovered from surgery.

Depending on how long the little boy was with her.

It bothered her that in two weeks she was already starting to think of him as a part of her. She'd spent every night at the clinic with him. And as he was going to be released to wait for his surgery date, they would naturally come back to the cottage.

"Do you have any children of your own?"

The social worker's question brought her back to reality. Only it wasn't aimed at her, it was aimed at James. Why the hell did the woman need to know if he had children?

Maybe because she wanted to know if other kids would be on the premises. Yeah, it could be that. In fact, the woman probably rationalized the intrusive question with just that intent. But in reality Mila got the feeling she was fishing to see if he had an ex…and children with that ex.

Because there was no ring on Evelyn Scott's left hand, was there?

She squinted a little closer. No, there was not.

A popular song came to mind, the dancing figures in a music video telling some unlucky guy that he should have given her a ring before it was too late.

Ha! James had given her a ring. For all the good that had done her. She'd mailed it back to him from Brazil, where it was better not to wear expensive jewelry.

Even if it had been completely safe, she still wouldn't have kept it. In fact, James had never acknowledged receiving it. Had the engagement ring even made it back to the States?

It didn't matter.

"No, I don't have children." If Evelyn sounded curious, James sounded peeved. Had he too felt the question was inappropriate?

"Well, it looks like everything is in order. And the cottage is adorable." Evelyn stuffed her papers back into her briefcase and snapped it shut. "I'll give my recommendation to the court that they make an emergency motion for placement with you. It'll just be temporary until we can file the rest of the paperwork. You'll have to let me know of any plans to move. And you can't take him out of state without permission."

"How about on a boat? Within local waters?" James asked.

A boat? What...? Surely not. Was he thinking of taking Leo sailing?

She blinked, trying to find some reason to be outraged, but she wasn't. She was happy. Happy for a little boy who'd probably never had the luxury of seeing—much less visiting—a boat like *Mystic Waters*.

Evelyn looked from one to the other, clearly a little dumbfounded. "I'll have to check, but I don't see why not. As long as you stay within California waters."

"Absolutely."

Mila had completely lost the use of her tongue, at least as far as forming words went. But she was grateful. Grateful for his willingness to take on a boy who was not his responsibility and provide him with a referral to one of the best orthopedists in the business. Not only that but he'd given the boy permission to live almost under his nose.

She stood beside James as he said his goodbyes to the social worker, assuring her she could stop by anytime she wanted. Evelyn nodded, flipping her hair once more and telling him she was sure she'd be seeing him soon.

As soon as the door shut, he leaned against it, blowing out a breath. "Looks like you're getting your boy. I hope you know what you're doing, Mila."

"I do. And thank you for everything." She hesitated. "Did you mean it about the boat?"

He nodded. "I thought it might be a good way to get his mind off things. Especially since he won't have surgery for another couple of weeks. We could even take him on an overnight trip to Catalina. It's still considered part of California."

Wow. He'd taken her to Catalina. And she'd been in awe of the beautiful island. It was everything the tourist pamphlets promised it would be. But maybe that was because of the man she'd had at her side when she'd visited it.

Well, this would be a little different. And Mila had to make sure that she didn't lose her head.

Not this time. Besides, he hadn't offered his boat because of her. It had been because of Leo. She had to remember that, and she would.

And she was definitely going to make sure she kept James at arm's length, because anything else was dangerous.

Dangerous to her. And dangerous to a little boy who would be looking for a father figure after the disappearance of his uncle.

Unless she wanted to risk Leo being as emotionally damaged as he was physically, that father figure could, under no circumstances, be James.

Now came the test.

"Are you ready?"

Patricia Stillwell slid a hand up to touch the stitches on her cheek. "I think so. Are you sure the scarring will be minimal?"

Examining the tiny stitches he'd painstakingly made, he said, "If someone knows it's there, they'll be able to spot it but, other than that, it should be barely noticeable. And a good makeup artist can erase all traces of it."

"What about the sinking you mentioned?"

Whenever there was trauma to an area, there

was the risk of fat cells dying off, creating depressions on the surface.

"It's too soon to know. If it happens, we can transplant fat from another area of your body into your cheek to even it out. We should know within a month."

"What about scar reduction surgery?"

There was that need for perfection again. If he had been Patricia, he would be more worried about what else her boyfriend was capable of. But every time James had tried to bring the subject up, Patricia had stopped him by either changing the topic or by defending him.

How she could defend a person like that was beyond him. Did she ever even ask herself why she stayed with him?

Then again, Mila hadn't asked him why he'd walked out on her. Even in Leo's room when he'd apologized for what he'd done. Wasn't she the least bit curious? Or had she just not understood what he was saying sorry for?

It's been six years, James. Give it a rest. She doesn't care anymore.

And he shouldn't either. But he did. Maybe he

felt the need for absolution. To get it all off his chest and have her say she forgave him.

Kind of hard when he hadn't forgiven himself.

"Are you ready to have the stitches out?"

"I am."

"Remember the redness won't completely fade until it finishes healing." Patricia had never had the problem of decreased melanin production in surgical areas that could sometimes cause the skin to become paler than the surrounding tissue.

"I've been through this before, Doc. I know what to expect."

She'd been through *surgeries* before. When he operated, he took the utmost care with what his scalpel touched and what it didn't. This was the indiscriminate slash of a blade without any concern for what it might damage. Patricia hadn't been through anything like this before.

And he hoped she never went through it again. The warning signs were there, though. If she didn't heed them, she could wind up back on his exam table. Or worse.

He gave a mental shrug. Not his decision to make.

Just like Mila's decision to apply to be Leo's foster parent hadn't been his to make.

Asking for the scissors, he prepared to cut the first of the line of sutures. He could have let his nurse handle this part. A lot of surgeons did. But he wanted to make sure everything was okay and that the scar didn't do anything unusual once the tension was released.

He snipped the first line, next to the knot. James was in the habit of tying off between each stitch so that he could control the tightness along the whole incision. It prevented stretching or buckling during day-to-day muscle movements or sleeping. It also meant that when he went to remove the stitches he had to cut behind each knot and pull the suture out section by section. But a good outcome was worth the extra effort.

And the outcome with Mila. Would it have been different if he'd put a little more effort into the courtship process, instead of rushing through it to get to the prize?

He had no idea, but he was getting pretty tired of having everything in his life bring something to mind about his failed engagement. And about Mila, who was now back in his life. To stay, evidently. For as long as the partnership between

The Hollywood Hills Clinic and Bright Hope continued.

By the time he got to the last stitch, he'd put his thoughts firmly on his patient and what he needed to do. Cutting the suture, he used his tweezers to pluck the tiny piece of filament from her skin, dropping it into a plastic dish that held the rest of the stitches.

He examined the skin, checking for any areas of weakness that might open up at some point. Everything appeared solid, the healing process well under way.

"It looks good." He reached for the mirror the nurse was already holding out. "Have a look."

Patricia peered into the reflective surface. "What about the holes where the sutures were? Will they show?"

"Some of that depends on your skin. But we've never had a problem with that in your case. I'll want to see you back here in a week to see how you're doing and check everything. If anything feels warm or starts to hurt, call me right away."

He looked up at her. "You know I'm not one to give advice."

Patricia raised her brow. Okay, so he'd advised

her against having additional surgery from time to time, but this was different. This was her life.

He smiled. "Okay, but it's only because I care."

It was true. He did care for all of his patients. It was how he'd gotten through his broken engagement and how he got through life.

"I know you do," Patricia said. "And I think I know what you're going to say, but I'm not ready to walk out on Allen. Not yet. I promise, though, if he loses his temper again, I won't stick around."

That was the best he was going to get. "I'm holding you to that promise. He has a reputation, and evidently there was more than a hint of truth behind it."

"Exaggerations. He's a great guy."

A great guy who cut open someone he cared about?

Yeah, well, hadn't some of his own patients raved about what a good guy *he* was? How good he was at his job? How compassionate he was with his patients?

And yet he'd been able to walk into a room where the woman he loved stood and slice her with words that would cut her to the core.

Some great guy he'd turned out to be.

Angry with Allen Claremont, with Patricia Still-well, and with himself, he gave her some last-minute instructions about scar care that would help keep the area as smooth and supple as possible. And then he walked out of the room and headed off for his next appointment. As he knocked on the door, he put Mila out of his mind once and for all.

CHAPTER SIX

"IT'S CALLED A SAILBOAT, Leo. *Un velero.*"

Mila smiled as the boy looked around in obvious awe at the pristine white surfaces of the *Mystic Waters*. She remembered feeling the same awe. But not about the sailboat. About James, when he'd stood across from her the night they'd met. The night she'd joked about toads and princes.

Her eyes had probably held the same wide-eyed wonder that night. She'd certainly let him hustle her off to bed fast enough.

Glancing at James, she saw he was watching Leo as well. Only he wasn't smiling. In fact, there was a solemnity in his gaze that took her aback.

They were supposed to be celebrating her getting temporary custody of Leo. Well, if the man's expression was celebratory, she'd hate to see funereal.

They weren't going sailing today but had made plans to head out to Catalina in a few days. But for now there was a picnic lunch Rosa had packed for them to enjoy. It was a rare day off for her, and for James, evidently, who'd managed to clear a large block of time to come out on this outing with them.

Why had he, though? Especially if he was so glum about being here.

Was he regretting letting them use the cottage? He'd been the one to offer it. And it had worked. The social worker had given them her seal of approval. And so had the judge who they'd met yesterday. He agreed it was in Leo's best interests to keep things as stable as possible for the moment. Especially when the child had the opportunity to have his surgery done at The Hollywood Hills Clinic.

She went over and nudged James with her elbow, keeping Leo in her sight. "Hey, is everything okay? We can skip lunch, you know, so you can go back to work."

It took a moment or two to get a response from him, but then the right side of his mouth tilted up. "That bad, huh?"

"You certainly don't look overjoyed to be here."

"Just thinking about how lucky Leo is to be

placed with someone who genuinely cares about him. Not everyone gets that kind of childhood."

Was he talking about children in general? Or about his own unhappy childhood? She knew that James and his father had never seen eye to eye. And there had been talk of his father's philandering in the tabloids. But in the days leading to their breakup he'd spoken of the man with a contempt that had floored her. And knowing about Freya's struggle with an eating disorder, she wondered exactly what had gone on in that family. She had her friend's account of fighting and angry words between the famous parents, but Freya had never talked much about her brother's interactions with them, only that he'd been left to practically raise her at times. Maybe Freya figured it was James's story to tell and not hers.

"No. They don't." This time, instead of nudging him, she let her elbow maintain contact with his arm, feeling the need to touch him. While the truth about the deaths of her parents had devastated her, her mom and dad had been loving and kind people. At least from everything she'd read and from her own memories of them. In that her aunt had told the truth. They'd also made sure she'd been well provided for. She hoped they'd be happy with the way she'd used their fortune, to better the lives of those less fortunate. "My keeping him might not have been possible without the use of your cottage. Thank you again for that."

"It's a small price to pay."

And yet he didn't act like it was a small price at all. In fact, Mila had noticed that aside from that first night in the clinic he hadn't touched Leo any more than necessary. He had lifted him onto the boat. But it had been a quick heave-ho, setting him on his feet. It had lasted all of five seconds.

"But it was a price you were *willing* to pay."

Unlike marrying her.

James's frown deepened. Because he'd guessed her thoughts? Time to change tack.

"Why don't we break into that basket Rosa packed for us?"

The furrows softened. As badly as he'd hurt her six years ago, she couldn't find it in her to lash out. Not now. Back when it had happened? Oh, yeah. She'd raged, written terrible destructive things in her journal for months afterward. It had been cathartic somehow. And now all she was left with was regret that things had ended the way they had. That he hadn't loved her the way she'd loved him. In reality, she should have guessed by the way he'd been acting in those last weeks that they weren't going to make it.

Except when she'd pressed him for reassurance he'd always given it to her. And once, while in a panic over the growing emotional distance between them, when she'd mentioned starting a family, he had murmured all the right things…told her he loved her.

Only those reassurances had been every bit as much of a lie as her aunt telling her that her parents had died in a car accident. Neat. Clean. Easy on the ears. But still lies.

Pushing back the tide of the past, she lifted the large picnic basket onto the folding table James had set up on deck, saying it would be nicer to sit out in the cool autumn sun than be stuck below deck. Besides, Leo was kitted out in a life jacket, which James had produced before she'd even had a chance to suggest it herself.

"Tienes hambre?" she asked him, as she spread the tablecloth, tucking it beneath the wicker basket.

"Si. Mucho."

James had introduced Leo to a pair of crutches, but since the boy was used to walking on his twisted feet, he'd quickly discarded them.

But watching him slowly shuffle his way toward them, his face contorting a time or two as he struggled to force his limbs to obey, Mila's heart squeezed into a hard little ball.

His surgery couldn't come soon enough.

James helped her get things set up. As soon as she pulled the last of the containers from the basket, though, her fingers brushed across something shiny and smooth. Peering inside, she saw a folded pamphlet. "What's this?"

"Something I wanted to discuss with you over lunch. Away from the clinic."

Was this why he'd suggested coming out to the boat? Her heart sank. She'd thought he'd been trying to give Leo a nice outing. Instead…

She lifted the leaflet, and started to open it, only to have James place his hand on it. "Let's get Leo's plate set up first."

A stray cloud caused a shadow to drift across the deck, matching the one that was sliding through her heart. Whatever it was, it was bad enough that he expected her to protest. Why else would he have wanted to get her away from the clinic?

"We could have discussed this at the house."

"I wanted to show it to you in a neutral setting."

Neutral? Was he kidding? This huge boat was anything but neutral. They'd made love in the cabin below—one of the reasons she thought James had wanted to eat up on deck. How wrong she'd been. He didn't see this boat as anything but a sailing vessel. As his property.

Fine. He wanted to talk about whatever was inside that pamphlet? She would surprise him by not reacting at all.

She was going to remain cool, calm and collected. No matter what James said or did.

"They want us to what?"

The horror on her face would have been comical if it hadn't mirrored his own feelings. This was exactly why he'd wanted to get her away. And knowing she wouldn't go anywhere without Leo in tow, he'd been forced to pretend it was an outing planned just for the boy.

Only that had backfired. Leo's obvious joy at being on his boat had made his chest burn in a way that it hadn't since he'd brought the ax down on his and Mila's relationship.

"You knew the clinic would want to plan some special events surrounding the fund-raiser for Bright Hope."

"Yes, of course. I knew there was some kind of ritzy ball coming up. But a regatta? Is that why you wanted to show me this while we were on your boat?"

He'd been just as surprised by the request. The parade of boats by clinic patrons was nothing new. They'd done that several times in the past. Except this time they wanted James and Mila to glide into the docking pier first and start the festivities off with a bang, since they were each the head of their respective medical facility.

"I thought this was a good place to discuss it, yes, since we'll be sailing in on the *Mystic Waters*."

James didn't like this any more than she did, but it was his responsibility to make sure this venture was a success. He'd put his reputation on the line for Freya's pet project and he had no choice but to see it through to the bitter end. Especially with Freya so close to giving birth to her twins.

He would let nothing hurt her, either physically or emotionally.

So there it was. And since it was actually his sister who'd suggested they arrive together—even mentioning James's prized boat to one of the board members when he hadn't been around to shoot the idea out of the water—he was stuck.

"Freya didn't mention anything about this to you?"

"Does it look like she did?" Mila cast a quick glance at Leo as if trying to make sure he didn't understand. But so far the youngster was busy making roads in his mashed potatoes with his spoon, making engine noises as the utensil sped through the white surface.

"If it makes you feel better, I didn't know about this either until just the other day. I knew the clinic was putting on a gala to celebrate our partnership, and we've held regattas in the past. But us arriving together was new."

"So you knew they wanted us to, but you're only now telling me about it." She flicked the pamphlet toward him. The same picture graced the cover that was on the wall at her new clinic. Promising an event that was "not to be missed."

"You couldn't have warned me before these were printed? What if I said no?"

"Part of your clinic's agreement with us states—"

"I know what it says. I signed it, remember? But I didn't know that it would entail playing dress-up and parading around in front of a lot of rich…" She cut off her sharp words and set down her fork. "I just want to help people, James. Maybe I should just go back to my little clinic in LA and do what I set out to do."

"You could do that, yes. But you would be letting down a whole lot of people. People like Freya." He steeled himself and went for the jugular. "Children like Leo."

Mila's breath hissed in, eyes widening in shock and dismay. "Is that a threat?"

"What? Hell, no. What do you take me for?" He dragged a hand through his hair, leaning back in his chair. "Forget I asked that. I know exactly what you think of me."

"Then give me a reason not to." There was an element of pleading in her voice—maybe about the past, maybe not. But the time for confession was over. Not that there'd ever really been an opportunity once he'd broken things off. Truthfully, he hadn't wanted to. The shame of the lifestyle he'd once led and the consequences of it—real or made up—and his own screwed-up family had made him choose to remain silent about Cindy.

He'd loved Mila too much back then to subject her to the ugliness that had gone on behind the scenes to avoid a scandal for his famous parents. When he had refused to go to Cindy and offer to pay her to have an abortion, his father had done so instead. Only Cindy hadn't been pregnant. But she had threatened to sue his parents and had even secretly taped the conversation between her and Michael, saying she was going to sell it to the highest bidder unless James agreed to marry her.

In order to spare Mila the humiliation of being dragged through the mud right along with him, he'd ended their engagement. And somehow the whole mess had just gone away. He had no doubt his father had shelled out some ungodly sum of cash to make that happen. By the time he'd found out Cindy had never been pregnant at all, Mila had been long gone, and James had never heard another word from her.

He realized she was still looking at him, waiting for his response. "All I can tell you is that the way this regatta was laid out wasn't my idea. But I think it could benefit both of our clinics. It's one night, Mi. Surely you can stand to sail with me one more time. Once we dock and go on shore, we can do the obligatory dance to kick off the gala, head to our own separate corners of the ballroom and go home unscathed."

She seemed to consider that for a moment. "It's not that…" She gave a rueful grin. "Okay, so it is partially that. But the worst thing is that you kept this to yourself until you couldn't hide it any longer. You could have trusted me with the truth."

"I had some idea of how you might respond."

This time she laughed. "Okay, so you got me there. So much for not reacting."

"Excuse me?"

She waved away his question. "Never mind. So we get on your boat in our black-tie best, eat a few hors d'oeuvres for the benefit of some wealthy donors, and then when the gala is under way…"

"Then when the gala is under way…we dance."

She shook her head. "We dance badly. So badly they let us off the hook almost immediately."

"The worst anyone has ever seen."

Mila picked up her fork and cut into her fried chicken. "All I can say is that you'd better make it look believable. And the bad dancer isn't going to be me, mister. It's going to be all you."

He laughed. A spark of the old Mila had just emerged from the ashes of the past, an energetic playfulness that he'd missed more than he'd realized. For the most part he'd seen only the professional self-assured Mila of the here and now. Except during those kisses.

Oh, she'd been knocked for a loop all right. He'd sensed it. And he'd been knocked just as hard.

That was one of the reasons he agreed their dance should be short and sweet. A quick, awkward shuffle that would get them off the floor as fast as possible.

If he played his cards right, not even the intuitive Freya would realize his and Mila's dance fail was anything other than the real deal.

She shouldn't dwell on how right James looked carrying a sleeping child. Because if things had been different, Leo could have been theirs. An ache settled in her chest that made it hard to breathe.

Not a smart place to let herself land. Especially not after the meal they'd eaten together on the *Mystic Waters*. Or after learning that they would share the opening dance at a fancy ball.

Just like the dance they might have shared at their wedding.

Leading the way across the dark rustic path that wound around to the back of James's property, she didn't dare close her eyes, even though the dull ache had turned into a jabbing spear that reached the core of her being.

"There's a light switch on the post to your right." His low voice slid through night air. Leo had fallen fast asleep during the car ride back from the boat, but when Mila had gone to wake the child, James had given a slight shake of his head. "The boy's walked enough today," he'd said.

As reluctant as James had seemed about getting involved, his words had said something different. He did care. So did Mila. Maybe a little too much.

But what was to stop her from eventually adopting Leo if his uncle was never found or if he didn't want his nephew? Even James had hinted at that possibility.

Too soon to think of that, Mila.

She pressed the glowing button on the wooden fence post and the area came alive with twinkle lights. Beautiful and romantic, the tiny overhead beacons glinted off the water of the L-shaped pool and made the small courtyard between the two buildings seem unbearably intimate. Her brows went up. Before she could voice the question, or even wonder if James had designed this place for seduction, he answered her question.

"Rosa likes to sit out here at night and drink her coffee. I didn't think she should sit in the dark." A flash of teeth from beside her. "*I* wanted to put in floodlights. She wanted something that wouldn't 'blind' her, as she so tactfully put it."

Mila smiled back. "I don't think the word 'tact' is in Rosa's vocabulary."

The housekeeper was warm and kind, but opinionated. She'd told Mila in no uncertain terms that she would do the cleaning in the cottage—and had offered her services to babysit without hesitation.

"No. It's not." He shifted Leo in his arms, and the working of his biceps made her swallow again. His free days had always been spent on his boat, and he must still do that whenever he could. She could remember how heavy those booms were to move, and hoisting the sails made her own muscles scream with fatigue. But she'd learned to love it, even though she hated to think what its price tag must have been. When they were out there, it was like they were in their own private world. A land of promises and make-believe.

Make-believe was all it had been in the end, though.

Kind of like this beautiful night.

They reached the front door of the cottage and she hesitated, not wanting the magic to end just yet but afraid to say anything, afraid she'd come across as needy and pathetic. They'd had such a wonderful afternoon. And those lights looked so peaceful…so inviting.

She forced herself to give him an out, though, as she turned the key in the lock. "Do you want me to take him from here?"

"I'll carry him to his room."

His room.

And that sounded just as right as the sight of James holding him.

"Would you like some coffee? I have decaf, if you're worried about it keeping you awake."

He glanced at her as he entered the cottage. "Do you have an early day ahead of you?"

So was that a yes or a no?

"I don't have to be at the clinic until nine."

"In that case, I would love some. Let me tuck him in and I'll come and help you."

Relief swamped her veins, although why she should care one way or the other was beyond her. She just had a feeling that tomorrow would bring something different, and she wanted the ease she'd had with him right now to last just a little longer.

"There's a video monitor in his room. If you could switch it on and make sure it's aimed at the bed, that would be great. The receiver is in my room." She hurried to add, "Sometimes I think I hear him crying and then realize it's just my imagination."

"I know what you mean."

He did? Since Leo didn't live in the main part of the house, she had no idea why he'd be thinking he heard him. "If he cried loudly enough for you to hear him all the way to your house, I wouldn't need a baby monitor."

He turned down the hallway, his next words barely audible. "I wasn't talking about Leo."

He wasn't? Then who?

Oh, Lord, maybe asking him for coffee hadn't been such a smart idea after all. There was a mine-field stretching between them that made navigating safe topics almost impossible. Because sooner or later... *Boom!* Something from the past would explode, sending both of them running for cover.

Or her, anyway. James seemed pretty impenetrable.

Except for that last inscrutable comment.

She'd just switched on the coffeemaker and was stretching up to reach for the extra coffee cups when an arm brushed hers, easily retrieving the mugs. A shiver went over her.

"Thank you."

"You're welcome." He glanced at the counter. "Rosa must have outfitted this after getting the news that you'd be staying here. If I recall, the cottage had furniture but not much else."

"You don't have people stay here? What about your parents?"

He stiffened for a second, before placing the mugs on the counter. "They're busy. I'm busy. But to answer your question, I think you're the first person who has actually stayed in the place."

Mila blinked. She'd halfway expected this to be his own private love nest but maybe his women stayed in the main house. In James's bedroom.

Of course they would.

Her stomach clenched. She pushed aside that thought and went back to the previous one. His relationship with his dad had always been rocky, but surely his mom had visited him in the time since James had broken their engagement.

The coffee pot gurgled as it finished churning out the last of the fragrant brew.

"Do you want to take it in here or out in the courtyard?"

He picked up the video monitor, glancing at the image of Leo peacefully sleeping. "How far does this reach?"

"The package lists the range as up to eight hundred feet, so that should give us plenty of room. If we start getting a lot of static, we'll come back into the house."

"I closed the baby gate you had in front of the door. Hope that was okay."

She'd installed the gate to keep Leo from wandering off in the middle of the night. She had no idea what his uncle had used to do at his old house, and closing the bedroom door didn't feel right to her. But James had a pool, and the last thing she wanted was for Leo to decide to go for a swim when she wasn't looking. Then again, she didn't want him waking up and feeling trapped. The gate had seemed like a good compromise. "That's perfect."

They each fixed their coffee, then James loaded their cups and some cookies that Mila had pulled from another cupboard onto a tray and headed to the deck that stretched between the cottage and the pool. A round café table perched on the stone patio and looked out over the water. James set the tray on the table and moved the chairs so they faced the pool. Mila peered at the receiver of the video monitor. There was Leo, as clear as day. When she thumbed the roller button on the side of the device she could raise the sound enough to hear Leo's soft snoring. No static at all. She turned it back down so that they would hear him cry but not every little shift of the sheets.

She dropped into a seat, while James went over to another set of posts, which had a hammock strung between them, and turned a dial. The overhead lights dimmed even more.

Sighing, she closed her eyes for a second, allowing the still-warm autumn air to brush over the skin on her calves, where the skirt on her sundress had slid up. She fiddled with one of the thin straps of her top. "This is nice. I would be out here every night, if I were you."

"I don't have much time for anything but work and sleep."

She nodded at the tanned skin of his forearms. "You have time for your boat."

"I sometimes sleep out there so it serves a dual purpose."

He slept there? When he had this beautiful home? Then again, she could remember spending some enjoyable nights on that boat.

Picking up her cup, she took a sip of her coffee. The warmth trailed down her throat and hit her belly with a splash of heat. "I think I'd be in the pool, floating my cares away."

He smiled. "Would you? I seem to remember you being afraid of water."

"Not any water. Just the ocean. You can't see what's down there. I've seen enough shark movies to know what happens when you venture in. As soon as the music starts, you're a goner."

"You do realize movie sharks aren't real."

"Of course I do. But sharks exist. And they do have teeth."

His grin widened. "You have more of a chance of—"

She put up a hand. "Save it. I already know the statistics. I've also read the stories. Seen the surfboards. It happens and I'd rather not be one of the few unlucky ones. Besides, if I felt anything against my leg, I'd be dead of a heart attack."

"Not everything that brushes against your leg in the water is dangerous."

She went still, very aware of that minefield she'd thought about a half hour ago. Did she dare take another step through that grassy field? Or did she retreat?

"No. Not everything."

"Did you bring a suit with you?"

She ventured forward another step, not sure where all of this was leading. "No. I didn't think about it."

She should have, though. Leo would want to go in the pool eventually. But she didn't think that's what James was talking about at the moment.

"It's still fairly early. And it's a warm night. Do you want to take a quick dip?"

Hadn't he heard her?

"No. Swim. Suit. Remember?"

Surely he didn't mean to...

"You can leave your dress on." He gestured at his board shorts. "And these are almost like swim trunks."

She was tempted. Oh, so tempted. He'd said they would keep their clothes on, so what was the harm?"

"What about Leo?"

He picked up the monitor. "Let me see if this reaches a little farther." He walked the few yards to the pool and nodded. He set it down on one of the lounge chairs. "Crystal clear," he said.

Her mind scrambled around for a reason to say no, although somehow she would be crushed if she actually found one. "Won't Rosa think it's odd to see us swimming around in our clothes?"

"Her bedroom is on the other side of the house. And the pool is screened from view, anyway."

Had he planned that to hide his late-night swims with bimbos?

Stop it, Mila. Just enjoy the night.

"If Leo wakes up—"

"I'll be out of the pool so fast you'll swear I was never there in the first place." He frowned. "Is he a light sleeper?"

Except for that first night in the hospital, he wasn't. In fact, he'd slept straight through to dawn ever since. "He doesn't seem to be, no."

"What's the problem, then?"

There was one. She was sure of it. She just couldn't find it at the moment, so she shrugged. "I guess there's not one."

James downed the rest of his coffee. "Shall we, then?"

Thinking this was probably one of the stupidest decisions she'd ever made, she set her mug down and stood to her feet, kicking off her sandals. Before she could put one foot in front of the other, though, James suddenly scooped her up in his arms and headed straight for the pool. In the daytime she would have shrieked with a mixture of laughter and alarm, but afraid she'd wake someone up she settled for hissing, "What are you doing?"

James didn't stop moving until he reached the very edge of the pool. "What am I doing? Something I haven't done in a very long time." He gave her a smile full of intent. "You know the drill. Hold your breath."

And with that he stepped off the side of the pool and sank, feetfirst, into the chilly water.

Taking Mila with him.

CHAPTER SEVEN

WHY HAD HE done that?

He had no idea. As Mila spluttered to the surface and then gripped the side of the pool, he only knew that walking into the house with that child in his arms had made his chest tighten. A sensation he didn't like. And then watching his ex-fiancée's hips twitch from side to side had made something else tighten. Something a little lower. Presented with a choice of which one to focus on, he'd gone for the easier choice: lust.

Something that jumping into a cold pool should have remedied. Only it hadn't. Because Mila's white sundress now seemed to have become almost invisible, every spot where it was plastered to her skin becoming pink and inviting. And there was a whole lot of plastering going on. In some very strategic places.

"Are you crazy?" She finally looked his way, eyes wide.

It would appear he was. Because instead of the water chilling any uncomfortable urges, it simply reminded him of another time in the distant past when they'd done this very thing.

Only there hadn't been any sundresses involved. Or any other clothing, for that matter.

He slicked his hair back from his forehead. "I was afraid you'd chicken out. And it *is* a warm evening."

Getting warmer by the second.

"So your solution is dunking me?"

"You were going to get in anyway."

One of the straps on her dress slid down her arm, carrying a wide swath of fabric with it. She hurriedly yanked it back up. "I was going to get in slowly. One toe at a time. But you didn't give me a chance to do anything but..." She glanced down, her words stopping. "Oh, my God."

She ducked down until only her head was showing above the water line. "Why didn't you tell me?"

The muscles on one side of his mouth pulled up. "I was going to once you stopped talking."

"You...you..."

One of her feet connected with his thigh, but

the water kept the kick from feeling like anything except a sensual slide of flesh against flesh. He reached down and grabbed the offending limb. "Now, now, Mila. I think we've been down this road before."

And they had. That kick had probably been pure muscle memory from the past. And every time it had ended the same way, with him gripping her calf and hauling her closer until the lower half of her was snugged to the lower half of him.

And like the crazy leap into the pool, he couldn't resist the impulses that were beginning to pulse through him.

He tugged.

And she didn't pull away. Or screech at him to let her go.

Instead, she hooked her heel around the back of his thigh, just beneath his ass. Like she'd done so many times in the past.

Pure need ricocheted through his system the second she connected with his flesh. He wrapped an arm under her butt, lifting and holding her in place as he pivoted, trapping her between the side of the pool and his body.

"Hell." He couldn't stop the word from exiting

any more than he could force a certain part of his anatomy to soften and recede.

Wasn't happening.

He could just touch the bottom of the pool so he concentrated on more pressing concerns. Like the fact that all he had to do was slide a hand beneath her dress, ease her panties to the side and…

"James…" Soft eyes met his, and he could have sworn he saw the same urgency in them that was thrumming through his body. "What are we doing?"

Leaning forward, he allowed his lips to trail along the moist skin of her cheek until he reached her ear. "What are we doing? Anything you want."

"But, Leo…"

His eyes skipped to the monitor that was less than five feet away. The boy hadn't moved an inch. "Leo is sound asleep. Parents everywhere are envious."

Parents? Bad choice of words, James.

Mila blinked a time or two, seeming to be torn between a couple of options. Then her heel pressed firmly against him, and all the waiting pressure points tightened even further.

He had his answer.

Their lips tangled in a fury of need that had probably been building over the last six years. The contrast between the icy coolness of Mila's skin and the molten desire he sensed in her kiss turned him inside out.

He hitched his fingers beneath her other leg and hauled her up so she could hold on. Which she did, wrapping her legs around his waist and looping her arms around his neck.

Leaning back just a bit, he smiled when her lips followed his, her wordless protest nearly making him forget what he'd been about to do. But the sheer fabric of her dress had been calling to him for the past several minutes and he couldn't ignore the siren song a moment longer.

He palmed her breasts, the heady feel of her nipples against his skin cutting through him like a knife. Whether her body's reaction was from the chill of the water or from need, he had no idea. It didn't matter. Because the whimper that erupted from her throat as his thumbs skimmed over the hard peaks said she wanted every bit of what he was doing. Of what he was going to do.

Her neckline was rounded and stretchy. Elastic. He used it to his advantage, allowing one hand to creep beneath the edge and tug until he'd exposed an expanse of creamy skin. His mouth watered.

Gorgeous.

Everything about this woman.

And what she did to him…

Hell.

She'd also been fairly vocal during their love-making in the past. And with that monitor just a few feet away…

"I'm going to need you to be very, very quiet, Mi, for what I'm about to do. Can you do that?"

She licked her lips. "It depends."

Instead of answering her, he leaned down and covered her nipple with his mouth, letting his tongue scrape over the tip.

She moaned. Quietly.

It ramped the simmering tension into a vortex that drove him to the edge of ecstasy. And despair. He forced it back.

Not yet.

But it had to be soon, or he wasn't going to make it.

Pulling back, he wrapped his hands around her hips and with a single quick movement lifted her up and out of the pool, parking that fine ass of hers on the concrete deck, her legs splayed on either side of his shoulders.

Very nice.

He scooted her bottom closer to the edge, then eased her dress slowly up her thighs, gulping when blue satin winked at him from beneath it. He followed the strings on the sides, expecting to find bikini underwear. Instead it was…a thong. How had he missed that when he'd been manhandling her behind?

He had no idea. But he liked it.

Liked that she'd worn it while out on the boat. Had she put it on with him in mind? She'd used to wear a much more chaste version of panties when they'd been together. Slightly sexy, but not outrageously so. Nothing like what she had on now.

But the thong matched the new air of self-assurance she carried with her. All the more reason why leaving her at the altar had been the right choice.

He frowned at the thought.

Mila had evidently "found" herself while they'd been apart. She'd probably done a lot of soul-searching about what she really wanted out of life and what was important. Maybe he should have done a little more of that himself. Yes, he'd loved the person she'd been back then.

But now?

Not something he was going to let himself dwell on. Especially now.

To distract himself, he concentrated on what was right in front of him. Not that it was all that hard to do. His fingers tightened on the string of her thong. "Lift up."

There was a second of hesitation when he wondered if she was going to change her mind. But maybe the past beckoned her like it did to him. She put her hands on the pool deck just behind her and pushed up. Just enough for him to tug the panties down.

And off.

He shoved them in the pocket of his board shorts. She wasn't going to be needing those anytime soon.

Mila's head swiveled to the side, glancing toward the monitor.

"Still sleeping. I checked."

And he had. Despite the raging need that coursed through his veins, he was very aware of their responsibility to that child.

Their...

Now, there was a funny word.

"This feels naughty." Her words were soft.

"It is naughty. Very, very naughty." His hands went to her thighs, thumbs tracing slow circles across the pale inner surfaces.

"When you do that, it feels very, very good."

"And so do you." He leaned forward and placed a kiss just below one of his thumbs. "Mmm...and you taste just as good."

A shiver went through her, and her hands went to his head, fingers threading through his hair. "God, I need you, James."

He cupped her behind as he propped his chin on the very edge of the pool, just inches away from where he wanted to be. "Then come and get me, honey."

Would she? Or would she chicken out and make him haul her forward? Where he could kiss her until those shivers became moans of desperation?

And hell if she didn't take the initiative and edge closer inch by inch until she was right there in front of him, fingers still deep in his hair. Tightening.

"Perfect. So perfect." He lifted his chin and ran

it along the place where the satiny skin of her leg gave way to a much more erotic zone. A place where everything was smooth and bare.

Another surprise.

In slow passes, he brushed against the silken flesh with his cheek…his chin…his nose. And finally his lips. Right at the heart of her.

When he glanced up her body, he found her head back, eyes closed as he continued to explore.

He couldn't get enough. Wanted to touch her with every single part of his body. He nibbled. Licked. Breathed. Everything he could think of.

Mila squirmed against him, using her grip on his hair to pull him even closer. And he was happy to oblige.

Her breath came in desperate-sounding puffs of air, the whispers curling past his ear and messing with his head. He'd told her to be quiet, but maybe he should have let her scream and yell and moan because this quiet, writhing woman beneath his mouth was doing something to him that demanded he pull her back in the water and finish it.

But not until he finished her.

Bringing one of his hands back around, he entered her with two fingers, pressing deep, while his mouth kept doing exactly what it had been. She was warm and wet and deliciously sexy. And he needed her. Desperately. Loved the pumping of her hips as she tried to find release.

Release he was more than willing to give her.

Suddenly, Mila's grip on his hair became frantic and she pressed herself hard against him.

There!

It came suddenly, in sharp waves that tightened and contracted and rippled against his fingers. He gritted his teeth and held on to his own need with everything that was inside him.

Because he wanted to be inside her.

"Now, James. Please!"

Wrapping his arms around her hips he carried her down into the water, shoving his shorts down in a rush and in one sudden move entered her.

A growled curse came out as he went deep, pressing her hard against the side of the pool as her body continued to convulse around him.

He couldn't hold on. Didn't want to. Needed her.

Letting go, he pumped like a wild man craving everything she could give him.

And give she did, her fingernails digging into

his shoulders, her mouth finding his and using her tongue to mimic what he was doing to her.

He gave one final thrust and wrapped a hand around the back of her head as he exploded, trying to absorb every sensation, drawing it deep into his mind…his body, his soul. His kiss slowed… softened until he finally got up the nerve to ease away. Even then, he let his mouth trail along her eyelids, her cheek and then back to her lips. Nibbling. Still tasting. Still connected to her.

"Wow. That was…wow." The soft words breathed against his neck made him smile.

Yes, it had been. For him too.

Something rattled at the back of his mind as his senses gradually returned. He caught sight of his wallet on the table next to the baby monitor. He glanced at the image of Leo, who was still sleeping peacefully, and then his eyes tracked back to the wallet.

His wallet.

Crap! The one containing his token "just in case" condom.

He pulled free of her in a rush, swearing in a voice that was the antithesis of quiet.

"What's wrong?" Her hazel eyes blinked in surprise, an uncertain frown contracting his brows.

"I didn't use protection." His brain sought an explanation and came up empty. "Damn it, I'm sorry, Mila."

How could he have done that? He'd broken his cardinal rule. But somehow the memories from the past—when Mila had been on the Pill and condoms had been an unnecessary evil—had clouded his thinking.

Maybe…maybe she was still protected.

She must have read the question in his eyes. "No. I'm not. Not anymore. Some of the places I travel…it's hard to get the prescriptions filled. So I just gave it up. B-but I just had my period a few days ago, so surely it'll be okay."

Surely. The word disasters were made of.

"You might need to make sure." The sentence came out before he could stop it, and his soul froze inside him. That was something his father would have said. Exactly like it, in fact. He'd said those very words when he'd told James to bribe Cindy. *You might need to make sure. It doesn't pay to take chances.*

Mila's reaction wasn't much better than his own

had been. Her words were small and cold. "You mean like the morning-after pill? Don't worry, James. I'm not going to saddle you with child support payments."

Hell, that wasn't what he'd meant at all. In fact the thought of her downing that pill made him sick to his stomach. But he was also worried about his stupidity costing her in a huge way. A life-changer. Wasn't that the phrase that was so popular nowadays to describe a catastrophic illness… or unplanned pregnancy? "I don't care about that."

But was that really true? He didn't care about the money. At all. But he didn't want to be a father. It wasn't in his plans. Not now. Not ever.

And yet…

No. Do not go there, James.

Too late. His mind had dredged up the image of Mila holding Leo in the back of the car as they'd made their way to the clinic. His eyes strayed to the baby monitor.

Mila shrugged, bringing his attention back to her. "Like I said, it's okay. Let's not make it into a national tragedy before there's a reason to."

It sure looked like there was a reason to from

where he was standing. What kind of birth control had she used with her firefighter?

Not a question he was going to ask. Neither did he want to picture Mila with anyone else, doing what they'd just done. Or wonder if she'd ever gotten so carried away that she'd forgotten all about birth control.

Like he had?

Screw this.

Before he could say anything else she hefted herself onto the side of the pool with one graceful push of her arms. And damn if the dress wasn't just as transparent as it had been earlier.

And double damn if his libido wasn't already waking up.

"Let's just forget this ever happened," she said.

He put his hands on the side of the pool and glared up at her. "You think it's going to be that easy? I don't think so, and I bet you don't either."

She stared right back down at him, water dripping from her dress and pooling around her feet.

"You're wrong. I can, and I will." She started to walk away and then stopped. Turned back around to face him. Squatted in front of him. "And just to prove it I'm going to do what the clinic wants and ride on your boat for the regatta."

"I thought that was already decided. And I think you're forgetting something."

"What's that?"

"I have something that belongs to you. Aren't you going to ask for it back?"

She cocked her head. "Ask for what back?"

James reached in his pocket and pulled out her baby blue thong. "This. Unless you want me to run it up the mast as my own personal trophy."

Mila's face turned crimson and she snatched the underwear and got back to her feet. "I bet you think every woman is your personal trophy. Well, guess what, James Rothsberg. Not me. I'm no man's trophy. And especially not yours."

Dropping Leo off at preschool was one of the hardest things she'd ever done. But one of the agreements she'd made with the judge was that she'd enroll him within the week. The rationale was that he needed to start learning English as soon as possible.

She knew they were right, but she'd still put it off until the very last second. The week was now over and here they both were, in front of the red-brick building that held Leo's well-being in its hands.

Would someone make fun of him? Bully him?

Her throat clenched so hard she thought she might suffocate. She understood that he needed to be in school, but why so soon? Why not wait until after his surgery?

Part of her misgivings had to do with James and what they'd done in the pool a week ago. She'd avoided him as much as she could, concentrating on her LA office, rather than the spiffy new one in The Hollywood Hills Clinic, even though she still needed to paint that damned mural. She figured that by staying away she could just forget he existed.

Not very likely. As much as she'd assured him she could put what they'd done out of her head, it was still there. Right at the surface, ready to rise from its watery grave to taunt her all over again.

How could she have let him have sex with her without protection? She was right in that her cycle wasn't at the optimal time for conception, but stranger things had happened.

Tyler had always taken care of that when they'd

been together. And maybe she'd let him because she hadn't been as invested in their relationship as she should have been.

But she certainly would have realized it if he'd made love to her without a condom.

With James, it hadn't even crossed her mind that they hadn't used anything. Until he'd freaked out.

And he had freaked.

All over her. All over her afterglow.

All over any possible child they might have. He'd made his thoughts perfectly clear. Having a baby with her was the end of the world. It should be for her as well.

And yet it wasn't. She'd bought the morning after pill and had sat it on the table in front of her along with a glass of water. She stared at it for the longest time. But she couldn't bring herself to take it.

Shaking herself back to the present, she drummed up her courage to let Leo walk up the path. The school had promised they had a staff member who knew Spanish who would step in if there were any problems.

And she was supposed to place this child in

their hands? Yes. Just like every other parent did with their child.

Leo's not yours, Mila.

But he could be.

The whisper was there. Just like it had been for the last two weeks. She tried to suppress it. Chastise it. Curse it. But it was still there.

She took a deep breath and forced herself to smile down at the boy, who stood beside her in his brand-new school clothes.

Only he didn't have shoes on. Just thick socks with protective rubber pads over his damaged feet.

"¿Estás listo?"

"Sí. Listo." He grinned back up at her, showing he was indeed ready to go.

How could he be so cheerful? He'd taken everything in his stride, and the boy had such a wonderful attitude that it brought tears to her eyes at times. He should be furious at the hand he'd been dealt. Terrified at being left alone in a strange place with strange people. Instead, he was fascinated by every new thing that crossed his path.

Like red grapes. And broccoli spears (which he called trees).

A mother and her son walked past them, the

mother glancing down at Leo as they strolled by. The woman smiled at her. A genuine smile. And the boy waved at Leo with a mischievous grin.

"Estoy listo." Leo tugged her hand.

He really was ready. Even if Mila was not.

So she trudged up the walkway, following the path that hundreds of other parents had walked at one time or another.

And prayed she was doing the right thing. For her. For James. And most of all for Leo.

CHAPTER EIGHT

JAMES HANDED HER the oversized scissors. She
took them, careful not to touch his skin as she
did. But she was very aware of his warm scent
as it surrounded her. A mixture of aftershave and
the ocean. He must have been on his boat the last
week, because she hadn't seen him coming or
going from his house. Which should have made
her sick with relief.

Instead…it just made her sick. Because she'd
missed him.

A ridiculous sentiment. Sure, they'd had a quick
sexual encounter, but thousands of exes hooked
up at least once after their separation.

Well, that had been their once. And now it was
over. She didn't have to worry about that kind of
tension surrounding them anymore.

Except she still felt it strumming through her
like the low throb of the engine on James's boat.

Like now, when he leaned down to murmur in

her ear, "Are you going to cut that ribbon or just stare at it all day?"

"Oh. Right." Her mind swung back to the present and the reporters and people grouped around a wide yellow ribbon that covered the main entrance of Bright Hope. Her head tilted when she noticed Avery standing next to Tyler, chatting with him like they were best friends. Was that why the other woman had asked if it was truly over between Mila and the firefighter yesterday? Avery deserved someone like Tyler—and he deserved a woman who could love him unconditionally. And there was no better time than this for new beginnings.

Today was the official opening of the clinic, although they didn't have any patients waiting yet.

There would be, though. Leo was going to be the poster child for the collaboration between the two medical centers. They already had a gorgeous picture that James had snapped of him on the boat, life vest firmly fastened as he stared over the side at the water below. The caption read, "Bright Hope was his life jacket. It can be yours too."

James had come up with the slogan, and Mila had to admit she loved it. The clinic gave the less fortunate members of LA hope and a place to go when no one else cared.

Well, *she* cared. Fiercely.

And she was going to make this work. Even if it meant working with James every day for the rest of her life.

Opening the scissors, she slid them over the ribbon and snapped them back together, severing it in two. The ends fell apart, metaphorically removing the barrier that stood between people and their access to this medical center.

Then people were surrounding her, shaking her hand, sticking microphones in her face and asking her to say a few words.

Maybe James saw the beginnings of panic on her face because he smoothly stepped between her and the throng of reporters and held up his hands. She had no idea what he said as her mind was completely numb, but it must have been enough to satisfy the journalists. They scribbled and filmed and talked to their cameras. And then they were packing up all their gear and heading back to the parking lot, moving on to the next big story.

And this was evidently a big one. There were still some fringe reporters—members of the paparazzi—hovering around the perimeter, hoping to get a shot of something unexpected.

"Come with me." The man she was hoping would leave along with everyone else was still here, holding his hand out for the scissors, which he in turn handed to someone else. A pretty blonde, who hovered nearby and seemed to know him well enough. Maybe a little too well. His assistant? His…what…lover?

He'd had enough of them over the years, according to the tabloids.

Maybe that's why the paparazzi were still here, hoping James would forget himself and give them a hint as to who his current love interest was.

She swallowed hard, trying not to let that thought sink in. It was none of her business. He could sleep with everyone in the western hemisphere and it should mean nothing to her.

Only it did. And she wasn't sure why. Maybe because of what they'd done.

Well, it didn't matter. They'd been over and done for six years. She'd be stupid to let anything start back up. Ha! Anything. Like sleeping with him?

She kept expecting him to check in about her period, to which she would respond that he should mind his own damn business. But he didn't. Nor did he ask her if she'd taken steps to protect them both afterward.

He never said a word about what had happened.

Which was good.

She thought.

Avery and Tyler came over, her assistant giving her a hug and congratulating her, while the firefighter shook James's hand. Her assistant had agreed to work at the new clinic, and Mila would be hiring someone else to take her place at the downtown location. The pair headed toward the parking lot with Avery throwing her a quick wink. Mila smiled back, hoping that meant what she thought it did.

James held the door, letting the blonde from the press conference go in ahead of him. Mila was tempted to just slink away—after all maybe that "Come with me" had been directed at the other woman and not her. Except James threw a glance over his shoulder that told her otherwise. He wasn't really her boss. She could just leave. But his clinic was helping her fulfill a huge dream: to bring the care she'd given in poorer countries to the poor of her own country.

Which meant she needed to suck it up and do whatever it took.

Including sleeping with the man who was instrumental in helping Bright Hope procure a premier spot in his clinic?

Of course not. The pool situation had nothing to do with business and everything to do with hormones and memories. Unfortunately the two had collided at just the wrong moment. Thank heavens she'd been able to separate the guilty duo and put them back in their individual corners. Which meant no more sleeping with this man.

Although the sex had been pretty damned amazing. And she didn't seem to have any real scars that she could see.

Maybe…

Absolutely not!

James was still holding the door, only now one brow was quirked in a silent challenge.

She breezed past him as if she hadn't a care in the world, only to run into Freya just inside. "Hey, I've been looking all over for you two."

The blonde was now nowhere to be seen.

"You have?" Mila had a bad feeling. Her friend had been so busy being in love with Zack that she hadn't seen nearly as much of her as she'd used to. "Why?"

James stopped beside her and tilted his head at his sister. "You could have just called me."

"I texted, but you didn't answer." An impish smile appeared.

"My phone was on silent for the ribbon cutting."

"Mmm-hmm. Sure it was."

What was going on? Freya was acting like there was some kind of inside joke. One that James didn't find particularly amusing.

Mila ignored him. "So you wanted…?"

"Zack and I would like you to be the twins' godmother. We've asked James to be the godfather, but since he'll already be their uncle… Unless, of course, you'd like to make that *aunt* and uncle."

A weird gurgling sound came out before she could stop it. She cleared her throat to cover it. What was Freya talking about? She couldn't be the babies' aunt unless she… Oh, Lord. Unless she married James.

Not going to happen. She'd already tried that once before only to have him back out at the last second.

But she hadn't completely gotten over him. The

pool proved that. It also made her realize that what had gone wrong between her and Tyler had probably had a lot to do with James.

In fact, every man she'd ever dated had seemed to fall short, damn them all.

"Mila, are you okay?"

She realized that both James and Freya were staring at her, James with an inscrutable look that made her swallow. He seemed just as unhappy with the prospect of her being involved with his sister's children as she was. As a godparent, she would be invited to all the major events of their lives. Family functions. Baptisms. Special occasions.

Weddings.

Mila cringed at the thought. What if James eventually got married? Would she be forced to attend?

It was on the tip of her tongue to say no, and yet as Freya stood there, blooming with health and happiness, Mila couldn't find it in her heart to refuse her friend's request. She came forward and caught Freya up in a hug, kissing her on the cheek. "Of course I'll be their godmother. I'd be honored."

Freya gave her a tight squeeze and released her. "I'm so relieved. You can't even imagine. Why don't you and James come over for dinner sometime soon so we can start planning?" She rubbed her belly in tiny circles. "Before I explode would be preferable."

"Oh, I…" She searched her brain for some reason to refuse but came up blank.

James tweaked his sister's chin. "Of course we will. Let us figure out our schedules and get back to you with a date."

"Soon," his sister insisted. Then her face went serious. "Bring Leo as well. When is his surgery, by the way?"

"In a little over a week." How had the time gone by so quickly? The child had been in preschool almost a week and his English vocabulary was already beginning to grow by leaps and bounds.

"Have you taken him sailing yet?" This time the question was directed at James. Why Freya thought her brother was responsible for Leo's care was beyond her. Maybe because they were living on James's property.

"Not yet." His voice had cooled a bit. But why? They'd taken Leo on the boat once already, although it hadn't left its mooring. But that had been to tell her about the regatta. It had been business.

Well, maybe they could make Leo's sailing expedition business as well. They could practice the route they would take for the regatta, getting the timing down. It was now only a week away.

She was already dreading having to get dressed up just to rub shoulders with people she had nothing in common with. But it was all part and parcel of what she'd agreed to. Leo would have his surgery just days after the gala.

She decided to broach the subject of doing something special with the child, not because she wanted to go sailing with James but because it would do Leo good. And it would help her get over having sex with James.

Exactly how was it going to do that?

By giving her a chance to be with him under ordinary circumstances. Besides, Leo would act as a chaperon of sorts. Nothing could happen if they had a child with them.

Ha! Leo had been less than fifty yards away the last time.

"I think maybe we should take him. We could run the regatta route and see how long it takes.

Besides, he won't be able to come to the actual event."

They'd decided to ask Rosa to watch him for the fundraiser. Mila didn't want to make any more of a spectacle of him than necessary. The advertising posters were bad enough, she didn't want him exposed to people who might be less than sensitive about his condition.

Thoughts that a mother would have.

Freya laughed. "Exactly. It would be great."

Said by a pregnant woman who would no more board a boat than she would scale a mountain.

"Again, I'll have to check my schedule. I have a medical practice to run," James said, the chill in his voice unmistakable this time.

She decided to ignore it. "I have to check mine as well, but surely we can both juggle some things in order to make this happen for him." She couldn't stop herself from touching his arm. "Nothing in this life is certain. Especially surgery. Please?"

She wasn't sure whether it was the "please" or the comment about the surgery, but the chill left and his face softened. "We'll work something out."

"Okay, my mission is complete. Let me know

about dinner." Freya started to turn away and then pivoted around again. "By the way, the mural looks great. When did you have time to finish it?"

Mila glanced behind the reception desk where the painting that matched the one at the LA location graced an entire wall. When? When she'd been avoiding James—that was when. But she couldn't tell Freya that. "I just worked on it a little at a time."

"Well, it looks great. I may have to have you come and do something in the babies' room."

"Anytime," she told her friend.

Freya put her hand on the door. "Did you find a dress?"

Mila blinked. "Excuse me?"

"For the gala, silly."

"Not yet. How about you?"

"You don't want to know." Freya glanced at her midsection. "Not that I'll be able to disguise this."

Mila went over and kissed her on the cheek. "You look beautiful, honey. I bet Zack tells you the same thing every chance he gets."

Her face went pink. "He doesn't exactly—um—*tell* me."

The inference made Mila laugh. "Okay, let's not head into TMI territory."

A muscle in James's cheek jumped. "Too late for that. And on that note I need to head back to my office." He paused to look at Mila. "Let me know your schedule."

Freya cut in again. "Don't forget you have to open the gala with a dance. Together." She threw them a wink and ducked back through the door before anyone could object. And Mila had a whole lot of objecting she wanted to do.

As soon as she was gone, James took a step closer, leaning his head close to her ear. The warmth of his breath sent a shiver through her. "Any more news?"

"News?" The shiver died.

"Yes. On our situation." He stared at a spot just past her shoulder. The fact that he wouldn't quite meet her eyes told her he wasn't talking about the regatta or dances but something else entirely. Still, the word "our" caught her right in the chest.

"Not yet. But, like I said, you're off the hook."

"I don't think so, Mila. I'm very much on the hook. And I plan on staying there until we know something one way or the other."

* * *

Two days later, James heard the news he'd been waiting for.

Mila wasn't pregnant.

Even as he feigned relief and did his best "that's great news" impersonation as she'd boarded the boat with Leo, something inside kept sending him withering glances. Which was ridiculous.

He did not want babies. Or any kind of child for that matter.

Even as he thought it, an excited Leo pointed as a sea lion popped its head above the water and looked right at them. And although James did his damnedest to ignore the sheer delight on the boy's face as his small hands clutched one of the chrome rails, he couldn't suppress the stab of joy Leo's happiness brought him. Especially when he ducked his head between the slats to get a closer look.

Mila squatted beside the child, murmuring something. Dressed in a white sundress that looked a little too similar to the one she'd worn in the pool, he found himself stealing glances at her flat stomach and imagining what it would look like if things had been different. But they weren't.

She looked relaxed and happy. Too happy.

Because she was relieved she wasn't pregnant?

Damn it!

He spun the wheel a little to the left to keep the boat headed straight down the coast and to take his mind off things he couldn't control. The trek was meant to take just over a half hour. So far, every second had been excruciating.

Time to do something about it.

From what he'd heard, quite a few of the boats that were to take part in the regatta were planning on decorating their crafts for the event. Whether it was white twinkle lights or elegant paper lanterns, it seemed everyone was planning on going all out. He was pretty sure the board expected him to follow suit with the *Mystic Waters*.

He glanced at Mila. "Maybe Leo would like to help us decorate the boat, since he won't able to come to the party."

Propping her chin on the rail beside Leo's head, he couldn't see her face, but her hand went around the boy's waist and she again said something to him. Leo turned to look at him, eyes wide. *"¿Eso es la verdad?"*

"Yes. I'm telling the truth," he said.

He should be dreading having to spend any more time with Mila and Leo, but today he found himself oddly out of sorts, and he didn't want to examine why.

Instead he focused on the here and now, and found he wanted to decorate the boat. Wanted to see Leo's face as dusk fell and they turned on the lights.

He wanted to see Mila's reaction as well. Speaking of which…

"Freya has been all over me about making sure my tuxedo is ready to go."

She shifted sideways, still holding on to Leo. "She's been asking about my dress color as well. And if we've practiced our dance. I wonder why?"

"Having the clinics join forces has been her pet project. I think she's worried we're going to mess it up somehow."

Mila glanced at him, her lips twisting. "Maybe that's why she's offered to go dress shopping with me. Do you think she guessed about our plans to get off the dance floor as fast as possible?"

"I haven't said a word."

"She knows us pretty well, though." She ruffled Leo's hair. "Maybe we should rethink things,

James. I don't want to embarrass her. Or either of our clinics."

"And how do we avoid that?" Mila was a good dancer. A little too good, as she'd always gotten a reaction from him. Then again, she pretty much got a reaction anytime she came within ten feet of him. Even now.

"Maybe we should make it good, rather than bad. Live dangerously."

He had no idea what had gotten into her, but he'd been living dangerously ever since he'd agreed to allow Bright Hope into his clinic.

"Dangerously isn't always the best choice."

Like forgetting to put a condom on before he had sex with someone? He forgot himself around Mila. He always had.

And maybe that's why she suddenly seemed playful and happy. She was glad he hadn't knocked her up.

Yeah? Well, he was glad too. And if the opportunity arose to have sex with her again, he wouldn't turn it down. He'd just be a whole lot smarter about the execution.

And if they danced for real? Would he be able to resist stealing a kiss or two?

Dangerous. Very dangerous.

Yet Mila herself was calling for a little of that very thing. Did that mean she was open to a few kisses too?

"I guess I'd better let her help me find a dress, then." Leaving him to wonder exactly what kind of dress she would choose, she turned back to Leo to point out another sea lion that had joined the first. Their heads bobbed in the water, staring at the boat.

"I think they're begging."

James couldn't blame them. He'd been known to beg for a crumb or two from Mila as well.

"They're out of luck."

Mila explained to Leo why they couldn't feed the pair. Tourists had learned the hard way by getting nipped by some of the more aggressive creatures. Giving them treats only made them bolder.

"We only have about ten more minutes before we get to our destination. Do you want to continue? Or do you want to drop anchor?"

Mila glanced at her watch just as a Jet Ski shot by them, hitting them with a spray of water as the craft turned sharply to the right. Both sea lions ducked beneath the surface.

"Damn it." James shifted to look at Mila and Leo to make sure they were okay before turning back to the idiot who'd cut a little too close to them.

Two people sat aboard the watercraft, and the driver was still hotdogging it, doing circles and zigzags that were more than dangerous. And they were a little farther offshore than he normally saw Jet Skis. It didn't mean they didn't venture out this far but they were almost a mile out.

Even as he thought it, the pair headed back their way, the person on the back lifting a can of something in salute as they raced past and circled James's boat, barely missing the *Mystic Waters'* bow before speeding away again.

They were going to hurt someone if they kept that up. He debated a moment or two about whether to let it go and leave the pair to their stupidity, but decided it wasn't worth the risk. He picked up his radio and turned the frequency to call the coast guard. Suddenly the Jet Ski cut too sharply to the right, sending the craft skittering across the water in a jagged course. It came back on center for a brief second but the driver must have over-corrected because the craft lurched to the other side and in an instant—still going at top speed—it flipped, tossing both of its passengers into the dark waters of the bay.

"Oh, hell!" Kicking off his shoes and yanking his shirt over his head, he yelled at Mila. "Shut the engine down and take the wheel. Radio the coast guard while you're at it."

With that, James dove over the side and into the water.

CHAPTER NINE

WHERE WAS HE?

Mila spotted one of the Jet Ski's passengers floating on the surface, life jacket in place, but the second one was nowhere to be seen. Neither was James.

But she had other things to worry about right now. Like getting the boat anchored so the light wind didn't cause the *Mystic Waters* to drift farther and farther away from where James was. She ran through the steps in her head, using memories of past anchoring to guide her: Point the bow into the wind. Pay out the anchor chain until it hit bottom. Set the anchor.

She wasn't going to worry about the setting part, and thank heavens that Leo's presence had made James decide to use the boat's engine rather than putting up the sails. She wasn't sure she could have gotten those down by herself. Putting Leo into a chair and telling him to stay there, she followed the sequence she'd set up in her head. Glancing back into the water, she still only saw the lone victim.

James was a great swimmer, but the waters off California's coast were chilly and visibility wasn't the best in this area.

The first victim, a woman, was now feebly paddling toward the boat.

"Can you make it?" Mila called out.

She didn't dare jump in the water and leave Leo—still sitting like she'd asked him to, although his eyes were now wide with fear—alone on the boat. She'd radioed a Mayday a minute earlier. The coast guard was on its way.

The person in the water lifted her head and nodded, long hair streaming down her back as she kept swimming toward the boat. Thank God she was able to move under her own power.

Still no sign of James, though. Her heart pumped in her chest at a frantic pace, trying not to think the worst. It had only been a little over two minutes, but it seemed like forever. God, what if something had happened to him? What if he'd gotten turned around underwater? What if...?

Something breached the surface, and she

grabbed the rail before realizing it wasn't a porpoise or, worse, a shark but James. And he had the second person with him. He sucked down several gasping breaths before his eyes met hers. Then, arm wrapped around the man's chest in a rescue hold, he swam toward the boat with powerful strokes, saying something to the other person as he crossed in front of her, but not stopping. There was an ominous stillness about the man he towed.

As soon as they came within reach of the loading ramp at the back of the vessel, Mila motioned for Leo to stay in the chair. *"Espera aquí."*

Hoping the boy would wait, like she'd asked him to, she leaned over the side and grabbed the second victim's arms, while James pushed him up from the waist. Within a minute he'd flopped onto the deck. She went into emergency rescue mode, vaguely aware that James had turned and was swimming back toward the woman.

A boat engine rumbled far off in the distance, but she didn't have time to look to see if it was the coast guard. Instead, she put her head to the accident victim's chest and listened. There was a heartbeat but the man wasn't breathing. She turned his head to the left, debating whether to flip him onto his side to give whatever water was in his lungs an easier exit, but the man probably weighed twice as much as she did. She settled for tilting his head to make sure his airway was cleared and then leaning down to start artificial respiration.

Between breaths, she chanced a quick glance at Leo, but he hadn't moved from his spot. And now James was helping the Jet Ski's other passenger onto the *Mystic Waters*, then he was back at her side. "Let me take over. The coast guard is almost here."

Mila didn't argue. Her first duty was to do the best she could for her patient and the best in this situation was to let James do the heavy lifting. She went over to the woman, who had sunk to the deck in a fetal position, softly crying as a cutter with official markings pulled up to the side of the boat.

Mila grabbed the line they tossed her way and tied it off, relaying the situation in brief phrases. "Jet Ski accident with two victims. We're both doctors."

Not waiting for them to come aboard, she checked the woman's vitals, which were surprisingly normal. She coughed up some water, and Mila helped her lean forward and clear her lungs, all the while trying to contain her own emotions.

She shared James's anger. It had been beyond stupid to race around like the pair had. It was a wonder no one had been killed.

Well…she glanced at where James was still working on the man…it was possible someone had been. As if sensing her thoughts, the woman looked up at her. "Is he…?"

Even after hacking up a good amount of water, the woman's breath reeked of alcohol, and Mila had seen her raise a can of something. It hadn't been soda, judging by how reckless the pair had been in circling James's boat. She bit back several responses before settling for something kinder than what she was thinking.

"James is a wonderful doctor. He's doing everything he can."

A choking sob came. "We were just out to have a good time. It was only our second date."

A uniformed man squatted beside them. "Is she stable?"

"For the moment."

The officer nodded and then turned to the

woman. "I need your name. Do you have any ID on you?"

Mila let him take over, glad to be able to get back to Leo, who had to be scared out of his mind with the frantic rescue. When she reached him she gripped the boy's small hand. What if he'd wandered off and had gone over the side while her attention had been elsewhere?

Anger pulsed past the relief, followed by concern. James, who was still busy doing mouth-to-mouth, stopped when the other member of the coast guard produced a manual resuscitator. He helped fit it over the man's mouth, and the officer began squeezing the bag while James felt for a pulse.

A minute later the man convulsed. Once. Twice. Then between James and the coast-guard officer they turned him to the side, just as he vomited massive amounts of seawater across the deck, gasping between bouts. But at least he was now breathing and reacting, and not the lifeless figure he'd presented moments earlier.

Once stable, the pair was transferred onto the coast-guard vessel. One of them shook James's hand and then hers, nodding toward the accident victims. "Thank you for your help. I doubt he would have made it without your quick thinking."

Mila shuddered. Undoubtedly. The man would have sunk to the bottom of the bay without James bravely diving in after him. For a few moments she'd wondered whether he would end up following the man to a watery grave.

But that hadn't happened. She had to remember that.

James's hair was plastered to his head, his strong chest bare. A rush of emotion went through her. A scary familiar feeling that sliced through her midsection.

It was just relief. It had to be. She couldn't let it be anything else. When she jerked her gaze back to his face, she found him watching her.

The coast-guard vessel pulled away with a last wave from one of the men, but still she couldn't pull her eyes from James's face.

Words tumbled out. "I thought you had…" Her eyes closed as another wave of emotion crashed over her. "When you didn't come up…"

She couldn't seem to finish any of her thoughts. Because they were too awful.

Arms came around her and a hand pressed her

head against his chest, holding her there for a minute.

"I couldn't find him." His words rumbled low and gruff against her hair. "I knew if I came up for breath, I'd lose my bearings and he'd die."

I thought you *were going to die.*

The sentence rolled through her head, but she didn't dare say it. Leo was still not fluent in English, but she didn't know how much he could or couldn't understand, and she didn't want to upset him more than he already was.

She let her eyes close, her cheek pressed tight against the coolness of James's bare chest, the reassuring beat of his heart beneath her ear.

He hadn't died. And he'd just saved a man's life.

When she finally let her lids part, she realized one of James's hands had reached out to rest on Leo's head and the boy's shoulder was resting against his right leg.

More emotion welled up inside her and suddenly she was crying, trying her damnedest not to sob out loud. But tears leaked and pooled and did all sorts of terrible things to her insides.

"Shh…" Something pressed lightly against her temple. "It's okay."

It was. Despite their past and everything that had happened between them. In this one moment in time the world had righted itself. It might not stay that way but for now she could revel in the fact that James was alive. And here. Holding her and Leo close.

She took a deep breath and let it back out. "Yes. It's okay." Before she could stop herself, she stepped up on tiptoe and kissed him, allowing her mouth to rest against his for several seconds before she finally pulled away. If she could have, she would have done so much more than just kiss him. She wanted him to take her down to that cabin so she could show him how glad she was that he was still here. Still alive.

But with Leo that was impossible.

And at the gala? The tempting thought swirled around and around like a wisp of smoke.

He'd teased her about being dangerous…maybe she should show him just how dangerous she could be. Trying not to let that idea get too firmly entrenched, she used the wide strap of her sundress to mop the moisture from her face. Not very successfully, though.

Not letting go of Leo, James reached over and

picked up his discarded shirt and handed it to her. She pressed it to her face, her nostrils catching and holding on to his scent. So achingly familiar.

She wanted another night with him. Just one more. Surely she could do that and then let him go. It wouldn't be an impulsive, crazy dip in the pool but a conscious decision. A reaffirming of life.

As if reading her thoughts, he stared at her for a long time, and then gave Leo's hair a quick ruffle and said, "What do you say we head back and start decorating *Mystic Waters*?"

James knocked on the door to the cottage two days later. Her nerves were twitching and fretting about what he would think when he saw her. Freya had dragged her to almost a dozen stores in search of the perfect dress. And Mila had to admit the red frothy off-the-shoulder confection showed off her figure to its best advantage. Rosa was already camped out in the living room ready to keep Leo for the night. A decision Mila had made on the spur of the moment after reliving their last few minutes on the boat following the Jet Ski accident. Something had passed between them as he'd held her, and Mila wasn't willing to turn her back on it quite yet. Eventually their interactions would cool down to business luncheons and quick nods in the hallway. But Mila—for good or bad—wanted that night with him…would feel cheated if she didn't get it.

She wasn't pregnant, and she already knew where she stood with him. He'd proved his inability to commit during their engagement, and from the various other women he'd been linked to in the tabloids over the years that was still true. And she definitely wasn't going to let Leo get attached to someone he couldn't trust.

He'd already been through too much, his parents' deaths eerily like her own parents' demise. She was going to ask to adopt him if his uncle didn't come forward.

It was the right thing to do. She was convinced of it.

The knock came again, and Mila sucked down a deep breath. Yes, it was the right thing.

And so was this. If James could have meaningless flings, then so could she. With him. Especially with him since there was no fear that he would press her for more, like Tyler had.

She pulled open the door and waited for his reaction.

It didn't take long. His eyes widened and slid slowly down her body.

"Wow." James took her hand and twirled her around in a slow three-hundred-and-sixty-degree turn. "You look beautiful. But, then, you always did."

She smiled. "Thank you. You look pretty good yourself. Then again, you always did."

Clad in a crisp black tuxedo, the man looked good enough to eat. And if she got lucky, she planned on enjoying every single bite.

"Are you ready?" he asked.

"Absolutely."

Something in her voice must have given her away because he glanced at her sideways, a question in his eyes. "What?"

"Nothing." Calling out a goodbye to Rosa, along with her thanks, she went ahead of him out the door. "I'm just planning on enjoying tonight."

He came up close behind her and laid a hand on her bare shoulder, his thumb strumming across her skin. "Enjoying? Or *enjoying*?"

"You'll have to wait and see."

"I'm intrigued. Care to elaborate?"

Despite her outward bravado, when they passed the pool her face sizzled at the memories that crept up. "Not right now. Maybe after the gala."

If she had her way, there would be no crowds, no baby monitors. No one but her and James. On that luxurious boat of his.

As if he'd read her mind, he murmured, "I'm going to hold you to that."

Climbing into his sleek black sports car, Mila settled into the leather seat, feeling a brief second or two of unease as the door shut behind her.

She pushed it back. She could do this. All of it. The party. The fancy food. The wealthy patrons. It was a price she was willing to pay to help people.

And if she held James out as her reward for sticking it out, she would get through the night just fine.

She was pretty sure James would be willing to go along with that plan. Especially after his last comment. The only question was how long they would last before one of them cracked. The way she was feeling right now, it might very well be her.

He backed the car out of the drive, pausing to

tweak one of her auburn curls. "You've let it go natural tonight."

"Freya thought it would go better with the dress than straightening it." When she had been in Brazil she'd tended to let it dry naturally, since she didn't always have access to the straightening iron she used in the States.

"I always did like your curls." One of his brows went up.

Was he remembering how she'd looked straight out of the shower, when they'd had unplanned nights of wild sex? Her curls had been much shorter back then, but he'd used to wind them around his fingers as they'd lain in bed together afterward.

She laughed. "Well, you have a bit of curl to your hair as well." She reached over and rumpled the waves just a bit, making them look wild and untamed. Oh, yeah. James was hot, no matter how his hair was.

"I still have to face my coworkers on Monday morning, you know."

"Don't worry, you can return to your stodgy old style tomorrow."

"Stodgy." He stopped at a light and reached over

to slide his fingers over her cheek. "Would you like to take that back?"

"Nope. Always were. Still are."

"I see I'm going to have to work a bit to disabuse you of that notion."

A shiver went through her. They were playing back and forth with their words like they used to in days past, only Mila wasn't quite sure he meant them the way she was taking them. But she hoped the sensual promise hidden in their repartee wasn't just in her imagination.

He might appear cool and polished on the surface, but beneath that sleek playboy veneer James had always been someone to contend with. There was a hard edge to him that excited her. He liked to experiment…and to play. And he'd driven Mila wild with need time and time again. He still did, in fact. Their sex play at the pool had been mild compared to what had gone on between them in the past.

They got to the boat in less than a half hour, and by that time James's hand was resting, warm and heavy, on her thigh, making her squirm.

The way his touch always had.

She was tempted to throw this whole damn

party to the wind and just drag him aboard the boat. Except they were scheduled to queue up with other watercraft for the water parade, and it would be pretty conspicuous if the lead boat didn't show up.

A few of the bigger yachts were hosting after-parties. She and James had already received multiple invitations, in fact, which James said he had turned down.

At first she'd wondered if it was because he knew she wasn't fond of all the glitz and glamour or, worse, because he didn't want to spend any extra time with her. But after his touch and words tonight, she hoped it was because he wanted her all to himself. Because she definitely wanted him. And if they hadn't had responsibilities to fulfill for their respective clinics and patients, she would have just chucked it all to the wind and hosted their own little party. A very private one.

But she did have responsibilities. As did James. But that didn't mean they couldn't retreat back to his schooner afterward and spend the rest of the night in that big bed of his. He'd once told her he'd never spent the night on his boat with a woman other than her, and she'd never seen pictures of him there with anyone, so she hoped it was still one of his unspoken rules. She didn't know why that was, other than a glimmer of hope that he considered what they'd once had to be special.

But not special enough to marry her.

She banished that thought, because this time she wasn't looking for marriage. She was looking to spend a single night with a man she was attracted to. A man she'd always been attracted to. And someone she was glad was still alive.

That made it okay. Didn't it? It wasn't like either one of them was hiding something from the other. They both knew the score.

By the time they got on the dinghy that would take them to James's boat, it was dusk and the schooner's white twinkle lights had already been lit. By the boat's caretaker, she assumed.

Since they would once again be powering the boat, using the engine rather than the sails, the lights up the rigging provided a beautiful profile. Someone had also attached white paper lanterns to the railing around the deck. They provided a soft light that made the teakwood glow. A glow she could see even from this distance.

The setting was perfect. More perfect that anything she could imagine.

Maybe she would talk James into mooring the boat out a little way from the rest of the regatta craft and when they were done with the party they could make love on the deck first, before moving below.

After all, they had all night. Something James didn't know. He knew his housekeeper was watching Leo for the duration of the party, but what he wasn't aware of was that Mila had taken her aside and asked her if she could stay the night, in case they got…delayed. The woman had kept a completely straight face and told her she'd be happy to, whether they returned at midnight or the next morning, and for Mila not to worry herself with letting her know one way or the other.

For all she knew, James just assumed they were going home once the gala was over.

Would he accept her suggestion of staying out all night instead?

She hoped so. The disappointment would be crushing if she'd misread his signals.

Maybe she should prepare herself, just in case.

Once James helped her aboard the schooner and

went up front to get things ready for the short trip, she did something she hadn't done in ages. She pulled her phone out of the small red clutch she'd brought with her and scrolled through her contacts. She'd added his number not so very long ago, since she knew they'd have to have business meetings, and so on. Finding him, her thumb hovered over the message button. Should she?

Since she wasn't brave enough to ask him outright, she decided to risk it. She quickly typed out the words. And before she lost her nerve, she hit Send.

James had shed his tuxedo jacket and had his back to her, but she could still see the moment he reached his hand into his pocket and pulled something out. His phone. He gazed at the screen for a second. Then he dropped it right back into his pocket without any reaction at all. And without typing anything in return.

What? Oh, no! He wasn't going to respond. Humiliation washed over her in a big wave. Maybe she could jump into the dinghy and take off before he broke the news to her in person.

A second or two later he turned around and

his eyes met hers. Too late. All thoughts of running fled.

She swallowed.

He came around the bulkhead, hands in his pockets as he made his way toward her.

Mila's face burned even hotter. She hadn't had the nerve to ask him about his plans for this evening, but he evidently had no problem breaking the bad news to her face-to-face. It would have been so much easier to get the message via text.

No, it wouldn't. But at least then she would have been able to hide her face until she'd composed herself.

And there was always the dinghy.

When he got to her, though, there was no sign of rejection in his eyes. Only some hot emotion that scorched her to the core.

He took a hold of her chin and tipped her head up. "Yes. I do have plans for after the party."

Before she could squirm away from him in renewed mortification, his cheek brushed against hers. "And those plans involve you. And me. And every available surface. Horizontal. Vertical. Upside down."

Her lips parted as realization swept through her.

He wasn't rejecting her. He was verifying every thought she'd had.

All that wordplay. All those little touches. He, too, meant this evening to lead to something more.

"I thought you were going to turn me down."

"I've never been able to turn you down."

Oh, yes, he had. She could remember one very specific time. But she'd made up her mind not to dwell on that. Not tonight.

This had nothing to do with their engagement. Or their past relationship. This had to do with want and desire and needing to spend the night with a hot, willing man.

The fact that she'd chosen him and not someone else meant nothing, except the fact that in the end James seemed a whole lot less complicated. He was a master at keeping things light and easy.

She shook off her thoughts. "How long is this party supposed to last?"

"I'm hoping it'll go on all night long."

Another shiver went through her. The man knew exactly the right thing to say.

"I might just hold you to that."

"What about Leo?"

"Rosa said she would stay with him."

He leaned back and a slow smile made the deep groove in the left side of his face come to life. "I see I'm not the only one whose thoughts were running in this direction."

One hand went to the deck railing beside her hip, while the other curled around her back and drew her against his chest. "If we weren't due at this damned event, and if we weren't quite so visible at the moment..." he leaned down until he was right against her ear once again "...I would go ahead and get this little party started."

He already had. Her insides were quivering with anticipation, nerve endings throughout her body going on high alert, waiting for the slightest signal that he was willing to set aside their duties and drag her below deck.

Instead, his arm uncurled from around her. Yes, it was a slow move, but it still had him moving away instead of closing the deal with a kiss.

Before she could draw another breath, though, his eyes met hers again, the soft lighting giving them an amber glow that reminded her of a wolf. "I plan on using the time at that fund-raiser to make you think about what's going to happen the moment we come back aboard. When I have you all to myself."

* * *

James had meant to drive Mila crazy with need in little ways. The touch of his fingers as he slid a champagne glass into her hand. The brush of his body against hers as he reached past her for an hors d'oeuvre. Instead, he was driving himself insane. They'd better start up the music for the dancing soon or he was going to drag Mila out onto that floor and make their own special music. One unheard by anyone except them.

He wanted her. Planned on having her. And this time he was prepared for anything. In fact, he'd peppered his whole boat with protection so that it didn't matter where they ended up. He'd done his best to ignore how it reminded him of his disappointment at discovering she wasn't pregnant. He should be glad. Celebrating it from the rooftops, but he wasn't. And he wasn't sure why. Neither was he so vain as to think Mila was a sure thing.

In fact, she was the least sure thing he'd ever come across. Maybe that was part of what drove his crushing need to have her.

He didn't think so.

In fact, if he let himself think too much, he might just come to a conclusion that he didn't want to face. And so he didn't. He let himself dwell on the pleasure that was ahead and dismissed any stray thought that didn't go along with that.

He'd had plenty of women since he'd broken their engagement. He would make this just another meeting of bodies. Only it wasn't, and he knew it. He still didn't bring women aboard his boat. But Mila had already been there during their engagement, so that didn't count. Right?

So why was it that when his phone had buzzed, indicating he'd received a text, his gut had given a knowing twist. And when he'd glanced down at the screen and read the words, his first instinct had been to text her back, jumping back to their former ways of ramping up the heat. In the end, he'd steeled himself against doing so. He hadn't sent a text for six years and he wasn't going to start now. And somehow he knew that if he sent her a message, things would go from a fun, superficial fling to something deeper.

But wasn't it already deeper? He'd slept with the woman once. Planned on doing so again.

His gut churned with a mass of contradictory emotions.

He didn't want to hurt her again. And after that pregnancy scare and with her moving forward with Leo, he was sure he would. So he'd done his damnedest to remind himself this was going to be all about the sex.

If he could just drill that through his thick skull and make himself believe it, he should be fine.

In fact, he knew he would be.

CHAPTER TEN

HE WASN'T FINE.

Over an hour later, there had been toasts and mingling and smiling acknowledgment of patrons as they promised funding for the next year.

James still hadn't danced with her. He'd watched her from across the room, champagne glass in hand, laughing with Abi Thompson and Damien Moore, both doctors who practiced at The Hollywood Hills Clinic. He and Damien had worked together on multiple cases, like Patricia Stillwell's, and from what James had heard, Damien and Abi were pretty much inseparable nowadays. Abi, wearing a dark green gown, stood close to him, smiling up at something the other man said.

A spear of some ugly emotion went through him at the obvious affection between them. Damien's hand went around Abi's waist, and she leaned into him for a second. She then held out her left hand, and Mila leaned closer to examine something on it.

Left hand?

His glance went to his friend, who even from this distance looked pretty damned smug about something.

Oh, hell, no. Surely not.

But even as Mila grabbed the woman up in a hug, her face alight with happiness, James felt something in his chest sink.

He'd thrown away something truly good. Something remarkable. No matter what Cindy or his father had done, he could have—and should have—talked it over with Mila. Instead, in trying to protect her from the ugliness of what had happened—the hopeless reality he'd thought he faced—he'd left her with no explanation. No possibility of working toward a solution.

She'd never asked for an explanation.

But then again he'd never offered one.

Maybe he should change that. Give them both the closure they'd been denied. Or it might even be something a little more than that.

Other people from the clinic had gathered around the pair: Flo and Nate, Freya and Zach,

Grace and Liam. All couples now. He should be happy for all of them, but the only thing he felt was a pit of emptiness that began in his stomach and spread to the rest of his body.

He decided it was time to go and collect his date, before he let the kernel of jealous longing ruin everything he and Mila had built over the last several hours. Besides, his hands and body were telling him to get a move on. She'd chatted with several other men. None had gotten close enough to touch her, but it had still sent an arrow jetting through his gut each time he'd seen her with someone else. Apart from that firefighter, James hadn't had to deal with the reality that Mila would one day find the man of her dreams. And start that family she'd mentioned long ago.

He would have to see them together day in and day out. Or at least for as long as their two clinics were housed in the same building. And since Freya had asked Mila to be her twins' godmother, it was inevitable that they would see each other over the years.

He wasn't sure he could stomach it. But she deserved all that and more. Deserved so much more than a man who'd broken her heart for reasons that had had nothing to do with her. And everything to do with him and his family.

Or was that just a cop-out he'd told himself over the years to avoid a painful discussion?

One he wasn't going to put off for any longer.

Maybe then he would be able to move forward with his own life. Whether that could ever include Mila was yet to be seen.

So he headed toward her, just as the small crowd that had gathered around Abi and Damien began to disperse. Abi looked relieved. He knew she didn't really care for loud, noisy places, courtesy of the PTSD she'd brought back from the war in Afghanistan. And Damien seemed pretty determined to make sure she was as comfortable as possible, leading her toward a private table a short distance away.

When James reached Mila, he found her staring off into space. But when she saw him, her pensive expression turned into a smile. Relief poured through him.

He let his own lips twitch. "What was that all about?"

"What was what?"

Nodding toward the pair seated at the table, he said, "That?"

Mila slid her hand in his and tugged him a short distance away. "They're engaged. She doesn't want anyone making a big deal over it, though."

"No. She wouldn't. I thought something was brewing between those two."

"Isn't it wonderful? And I think something might be starting up between Avery and Tyler. Did you see them at the ribbon-cutting ceremony?"

"I didn't notice." James looked at her with new eyes. Even with the disillusionment he'd handed her six years ago, she could still find it in her heart to be genuinely happy for others who found love.

Time to think about something else. Something that would take his mind off the obvious happiness of the newly engaged couple and put it squarely back on the woman in front of him.

"Speaking of wonderful..." He swept an arm around her waist and took her hand in his. "Dance with me."

She laughed. "The music hasn't started yet."

"Then let's change that." He moved over to where the DJ was busy getting things in order and asked him to start the dancing.

The man smiled and then pulled his microphone over, flipping through a chart of some kind. "Let's open up the floor for the first dance of the evening, featuring the heads of the newly merged Bright Hope Clinic and The Hollywood Hills Clinic. Here's to a long and healthy relationship." Probably having no idea of the irony of that statement, the man then held his arm out and a spotlight came up, capturing James and Mila in its glare. "Here to get this show under way is our very own Dr. James Rothsberg and Dr. Mila Brightman."

A round of applause grew and soon became organized into a synchronized rhythm that ended in laughter when James held out his hand, palm uplifted.

Mila obliged by taking it and letting him sweep her onto the dance floor.

They came together, a relearning of things forgotten, although James could swear he'd forgotten nothing about her. One thing he recalled with painful clarity, though: how it felt to have her in his arms. And how he never wanted to let her go.

So he wouldn't. At least not for this dance. Or the next.

Mila settled her hips close to his and laid her cheek on his shoulder. Her scent flooded his nostrils, and he strained to capture it, allowing it to seep into every pore. When she shifted and draped her arms around his neck, everything inside him tightened. He wanted nothing more than to whisk her away and show her how special she was. Show her how much he…

Loved her.

He took a hit to the midsection. Then another.

Why was he so surprised? He'd always loved her. From the moment he'd laid eyes on her he'd known she was someone who would rock his world.

And rock it she had.

The first song went by and soon other couples joined them on the dance floor. He spied Freya across the room, standing next to Zack, one hand on her belly and her other around her husband. She gave a little wave that seemed far too gloating.

Gloating about what? Him dancing with Mila? She'd known they were supposed to have the first dance.

His sister had been furious when he'd walked

out on Mila, and rightly so. Maybe this was his chance to make up for past wrongs. He and Mila could surely wind up as friends once all was said and done.

Except he loved her.

Was it possible to love her and be happy with just friendship? He didn't know. But what he did know was that he wanted her in a way he'd never wanted anyone else. And she wanted him. At least that text she'd sent on the boat would seem to indicate she did.

It was worth the risk.

He spun her around, until he couldn't see Freya and Zack anymore. Or Damien and Abi. Or anyone else from the clinic. All he could see was Mila. Along with everything she made him feel.

And suddenly it was enough. At least for tonight. Tomorrow? He had no idea, but he could make those kinds of decisions later.

"Hey," he murmured, allowing his lips to trail over her ear, suddenly not caring if anyone saw the move. "How much longer do we have to stay?"

Mila shuddered against him, her fingers tightening on his neck. "I'm pretty sure we've fulfilled our duty."

When he moved lower, allowing his teeth to nip at the long lines of her neck, she actually gasped out loud.

He smiled. "I haven't fulfilled anything yet. But I fully intend to."

When she pressed her hips against him, finding the throbbing, aching truth of the matter, he knew he didn't want to wait a moment longer. "Let's go."

Grabbing her hand, he hauled her through the clusters of people, throwing stiff smiles toward a few who got between him and the door and deftly maneuvering around them.

Then they were free. Outside in the cool night air. The second they were in his dinghy, he leaned over her, lips feathering across hers in a kiss that made her moan. Her fingers gripped the sides of the boat.

"That's right, honey. Hang on tight. This is going to be the fastest crossing you've ever made."

A tickly, scratchy sensation ran down one side of her spine. Then back up the other side. Mila squirmed, then groaned and rolled onto her back. The same prickly object flowed between her breasts, down her sternum, over her belly, picking up speed as it headed toward her…

Her breath caught just as her eyes flew open.

"James!" She half laughed, half screamed as she tried to get her bearings.

He looked up at her, his whiskery chin planted just below her belly button, an impish, unapologetic look of need in his eyes.

"I love hearing you say my name." Every word he spoke made those morning bristles scratch across her skin in the most delicious way.

She giggled, her body already heating as memories began flooding over her.

His boat. They were on James's sailboat. And what they'd done last night—well, she'd never forget a single second of it.

She turned her head in a rush to see if they'd actually…

Yes. They evidently had. Both posts of the headboard boasted a coil of rope. Burned into her mind was the exact second he'd released her hands so she could…

He rubbed his chin against her once more, slipping an inch or two farther south. She stopped him with a hand to the back of his head, managing to ask, "What time is it?"

"Still early."

It was? Because she could see light pouring into the cabin. "How early?"

"Just after seven."

Mila relaxed. At least it wasn't ten or eleven. In fact, if it was seven, that meant they'd gone to bed just three hours earlier. No, not gone to bed—because that had been hours ago. They'd finally gone to *sleep* at around four o'clock.

"Still, I have to get back to the house before Rosa worries."

"I called her and told her we'd decided to stay over. It was late and we'd both had a few drinks." He slid to lie beside her, still naked, his taut body making her feel positively drunk. "Besides, I wanted to talk to you for a few minutes before we go back to the real world."

The real world. Where life was not quite as fun and free of complications as it had been last night.

She turned to look at where he lay, his golden head pressing deep into the crisp white pillow. "If it's about…earlier…we used something this time, so we should be good."

"It was definitely good. In fact…"

"Again?" They'd used more than one of those condoms he'd brought.

"Is that a no?"

"No. It's definitely not." James had always been an insatiable lover. And once had never seemed to be enough with him. It made her heart warm in ways she didn't want to think about.

He reached up and wrapped a strand of her hair around his finger and then kissed the tip of her nose. "I have something I want to tell you. Something…" He paused as if trying to find just the right words. "I've been doing some thinking while you slept. I want things to be different between us this time."

This time? Was he saying…?

Maybe it was the same thing she'd been thinking for the last couple of hours.

A bubble of happiness rose to the surface. Maybe the past really could be rewritten. Or, if not rewritten, edited so that what had been a stark, dead ending could be erased, allowing for something better. Sweeter.

So, without waiting for him to say anything else, Mila slid her hands up James's chest until she reached his shoulders and then she gave a light shove, flipping him onto his back on the huge bed. The puzzlement on his face was as plain as the ropes that were still attached to the headboard.

Those cords gave her an idea.

Talking could wait. They had time. Plenty of time.

She took one of his hands and raised it above his head and then straddled his hips, feeling a definite nudge of reaction from somewhere below. Leaning over, she took the length of rope and wound it around his wrist, tying it just tight enough that he wouldn't be able to pull it loose.

"Hey, I'm trying to have a rational conversation here." The protest was halfhearted at best.

"Kind of busy right now."

"What are you doing?" He tugged against the binding, but one side of his mouth quirked.

"Isn't it obvious?" She took his other hand, feeling no resistance this time as she fastened it to the other side of the bed.

The boat rolled slightly to the left.

"And if we sink?" His pupils widened with lust and something a little more profound. Something she didn't want to explore right now. So she bit his lip enough to sting. His breath hissed in and he tried to reach her, but his hands quickly reached the end of their tethers.

"Oh, I'm counting on you sinking, James." She gave a husky laugh. "All the way to the bottom. And I'm going to enjoy every single inch as you do."

CHAPTER ELEVEN

LEO WAS ALREADY out and intubated.

Sitting in the observation room where Adam Walker was preparing to operate, Mila leaned forward, resting her elbows on her knees as she gazed at the scene. "The surgeon said he'll have to wear casts for four months and then braces for probably the next two years."

Adam had told him the same thing when he'd asked. The sad thing was that if Leo had been treated right after birth, while his bones had still been soft and pliable, the doctors might have been able to manipulate his feet into the correct position and held them there using the Ponseti method of casting and bracing. His Achilles tendons might have needed to be lengthened through a quick surgery, and the tendon which was attached to his second toe might have had to be transferred to his third to prevent the foot from re-rotating into the club position, but it was nothing like what the boy was now facing.

As it was, the muscles in his calves would have to be lengthened, as would his tendons to help rotate his feet into the correct position. And Leo would have to learn to walk all over again on his newly corrected feet.

He moved his glance from what was happening in the operating room and put it on Mila, who now had her chin propped in her hands, her muscles tense as she stared at the scene below.

Before he could stop himself, his hand went to her back, his thumb sweeping in gentle circles. He would give anything to take her worry on himself. But he couldn't do that any more than he could ask Adam to operate on him instead of Leo.

And he still hadn't talked to Mila, like he'd promised himself he would. But he needed to, and soon, if he wanted to have a future with her.

He did. Those thoughts had come slowly, but they'd been building with every hour that had passed. They'd spent almost every waking moment together over the last two days, he and Mila and Leo. And for the first time he'd wondered if he actually could have a family. If he could actually be the stand-up guy he hadn't been six years ago.

That would depend on how Mila reacted to what he told her. But first they had to get through this surgery.

Mila drew in a deep breath and blew it back out, then sat up, holding her hand out, palm up, to him. He reached across and gripped it, his other arm wrapping around her shoulders and drawing her against him.

"It's going to be all right." He forced the words from his mouth, more to reassure her than because he really believed them. Oh, he believed that Leo was going to be okay. That he would have a long and happy future. But he and Mila?

Of that he wasn't so sure.

They sat there like that for what seemed like hours, listening as Adam crisply enunciated each step of the surgery into the overhead microphone.

It seemed to take hours. It did, in fact. And yet there was no place James would rather be than sitting here next to Mila.

Finally, the surgeon stood upright and stretched his back. "That's it, ladies and gentlemen. I'm going to close and then we can wake him up."

Just as he took the threaded needle from one of the surgical nurses and leaned over the boy, an alarm went off. Then another.

"Pressure's dropping." The anesthesiologist's voice cut through the celebratory mood like a guillotine.

"What the hell's happening, Ron?" Adam asked the other doctor.

"I have no idea. He was stable a second ago. Give me a minute."

James's muscles went on high alert just as Mila stood and rushed over to the window, pressing her hands against it.

Adam, probably catching the sudden movement, glanced up at them, his jaw tight as he spoke into the microphone that linked the operating room with the observation area. "Get her out of there, James."

There was no way in hell he was going to tell Mila to leave. But if things got really bad, he would carry her out bodily if he had to.

By now the team was on high alert, Leo's feet forgotten as they fought to stabilize his condition.

Damn it!

"What's happening?" He knew Mila didn't expect an answer to her question any more than Adam had expected one from Ron Palmer, head of anesthesia at The Hollywood Hills Clinic.

Sedation was a tricky balance of drugs. Every person was different and the tiniest variation in the way the medication interacted with a patient could have devastating consequences.

Instrument tables were shoved aside and a crash cart wheeled in, just in case.

Hell, he hoped it didn't come to that.

"Let's get him stable, people." The strain in Adam's voice came through loud and clear.

Everyone was already working to do just that, but the alarms continued, unrelenting.

"He's tachy at one-thirty."

Leo's heart was beating too fast. They wouldn't know if it was a reaction to the anesthesia or something else until after they got things back under control.

"V-tach!"

Mila's whole body was now pressed against the glass. "Oh, God!"

If they couldn't get Leo's heart back into normal rhythm, it could spiral down into ventricular fibrillation, the leading cause of cardiac arrest and death.

His eyes burned and his gut was sending up alarm bells of its own. But when he tried to draw Mila away from the window, she shook him off.

"Don't touch me."

Just as suddenly, she spun toward him and wrapped her arms around his waist. "I'm sorry. So sorry. He trusted me. I told him it would be okay."

Mila had trusted James once upon a time, only to have him betray that trust so he didn't try to placate her or reassure her. He just held her and joined his fear to hers and hoped it was enough to ward off whatever was happening in that room.

The alarms switched off just as suddenly as they'd sounded, and everyone seemed to hold their collective breath.

Mila turned back toward the room below, one hand over her mouth.

"And we're back in sinus." The anesthesiologist's voice, full of relief, verified that things were turning around. "It's holding. Pressure's back up to ninety over sixty. Let's get this done."

James tightened his grip on her, kissing the

top of her head in relief. If Leo got through this, James was going to spill everything. Tell Mila the truth and ask for a second chance.

Adam worked quickly to suture up the surgical sites and finish his work while Ron kept his eyes glued to the monitors. Ten minutes later the surgeon peeled off his gloves. "Thank God. Let's wake him up."

Mila and James waited with everyone else as Ron eased the sedation. Within a few minutes Leo's eyelids flickered and then opened. The anesthesiologist put his hand on the boy's forehead and said something to him. Leo nodded.

"Thank God." Mila breathed the same words the surgeon had, her whole body sagging as she fell back into one of the plush chairs. "What just happened?"

"I don't know. I'm sure Adam will want to keep an eye on him until the anesthesia has worn off completely."

"I'm going down there." She stood as if she was going to do exactly what she'd said.

"No, Mila. You're not. Not until Adam says you can." They both knew the protocol, and James was not about to break it and risk Leo's life if something happened.

"But—"

He slid an arm around her waist, ignoring all the jabs his conscience was now giving him. "We'll both go. But not until Adam gives us the green light. What we can do is wait for him to come out and talk to us."

So they went down to the waiting area, Mila perched at the very edge of a chair, while James paced in front of her.

After what seemed like hours Adam pushed through the door. "Before either of you says anything, he's stable. He's awake and talking, but I want to give him a half hour before we add more people to the mix."

Meaning he didn't want them in there right now.

"You're sure he's okay?"

"Yes. I'll have the nurse come out as soon as we're ready for you. I want to run a few tests, but I think what you saw in there was a reaction to the anesthesia. It's rare, but it happens."

"We almost lost him." The words were out of his mouth before he could stop them. Mila's head jerked around to look at him, as did Adam's, except the orthopedist, known for his calm demeanor and unflappable nature, barely lifted an eyebrow at his outburst.

"It didn't come to that. My team was on it at the first hint of trouble."

James realized his friend could have taken his words as a criticism. "Your team is top-notch. I appreciate all you've done."

"So do I. Thank you." Mila held out her hand.

Adam gave it a quick squeeze. "Everything we did in there was a success. Leo will need bracing for a while, but he has a great shot at having normal function in both feet. We may need to tweak the tendons and muscles a bit as he grows, but those will be minor procedures under local anesthesia. Nothing like today."

"Thank you, again."

Adam nodded. "Let me get back to him."

We almost lost him. James's words echoed through Mila's skull.

They could have. And when she thought of all the lost years she and James could have had, she felt sick.

Suddenly she had to know.

She turned to him. "You said on the boat you had something to tell me."

"Yes."

"Is it something about the past? Or something about the present?"

His throat moved. "Both."

"Okay. I want to do this now. Before we go back to see him."

He hesitated. "I don't think this is the right time."

"It's the perfect time." She needed to know. Know whether they were going to be moving forward as a couple or if their lovemaking had been nothing more than passing a few hours. When she faced Leo, she wanted to know the score. Was she doing this on her own? Or did James want to move back into her life? And if she could get past all of their differences, she wanted reassurance that he was there to stay. Which meant she had to understand the past. "Let's start with ancient history. What went wrong six years ago? I want the truth."

The waiting room was empty, but James still pulled her toward the back corner and waited until she sat down. He remained standing, hands pressed deep into his pockets.

"The truth. Okay, my calling things off that day had nothing to do with you. Or my feelings at the time."

She'd avoided the "why" question for years, allowing both her anger and what had happened with her aunt to cloud her thinking. But if it had had nothing to do with how he'd felt about her...

All sorts of alternate scenarios began running through her head. Some of them outrageous. Some of them horrifying.

"So it wasn't because you didn't love me."

"No."

Had he been unfaithful? All those tabloid stories flashed through her head.

She clasped her hands in her lap, suddenly as afraid as she'd been during Leo's surgery. "Okay, then. Tell me why."

James's eyes closed for a second before reopening. "A former girlfriend told me she was pregnant."

The words meant nothing to her for a second or two, then realization dawned. Pain knifed through her abdomen, quickly turning to churning nausea. "You got someone pregnant while we were engaged?"

He knelt down and grabbed her hands. "No. Cindy and I were over a week before you and I danced that first time. Then things happened so fast, our relationship...everything." He shook his head. "A few weeks before our wedding day she came to me and said she was expecting."

He paused. "I didn't know what to do, knew that a media firestorm would break out as soon as word got out. I waited and waited, hoping some kind of solution would come to me, but there was nothing. So I decided the only thing I could do was break off our engagement, to protect you as best I could from what was about to happen. I'm sorry, Mila. Truly sorry."

The words swirled and danced, looming and receding before her eyes until they were mere pinpoints.

Then something ugly rose as one phrase rang through her ears. "You wanted to protect me? Protect? Me?"

Okay, so she was repeating herself. But it was because the same words were now slamming against her insides like huge lapping waves that threatened to drown her.

Only this time the words were from another source. From her aunt when a sobbing seventeen-year-old Mila had waved a yellowed newspaper in front of her face, the headlines an accusation.

I was just trying to protect you.

What her aunt had done, though, had been to rob her of a chance to see her mom one last time… to say goodbye.

James had robbed her too.

Mila swallowed the bitterness that coated her throat. More than once. Even so, her next words came out as a whisper. "You should have told me the truth."

She wasn't sure if she was talking to James or her aunt's ghost.

"I wasn't thinking straight at the time, and I truly believed she was pregnant. I felt I had…a responsibility toward her, and I didn't want you to have to suffer for it."

I was just trying to protect you.

He didn't say the words this time, but they kept echoing all around her.

"And what about your responsibility toward

me? I didn't need protecting. I needed the truth. *Deserved* the truth. Instead, you let me think I wasn't..." She brushed his hands away and stood up. Her skin crawled at the similarities between what her aunt had done and what he had.

"I did what I thought was right at the time."

I just wanted to protect you.

She shook off the words.

"What happened to the baby?" She turned away, not wanting to see his eyes when he told her.

"There was no baby. It was all a lie."

God.

It was. But not just one lie. More like an entire pack of them, circling around lost chances and stolen moments and trapping them inside—only pausing long enough to snap and growl whenever anything got too close.

A mishmash of betrayal, anger, fear and so many other emotions began crowding her mind, all vying for first place in her thoughts. She needed to get away. To think. To breathe. And she couldn't do that with James standing five feet away.

Before she could ask him to leave, though, a

nurse headed their way. "You can go back and see Leo. He's asking for you. Both of you."

She did the only thing she could. Without looking to see if James was following, she gritted her teeth to hold back the cry of pain and walked down the long hallway.

Mila was aware of the second Leo opened his eyes and looked at her. Her heart went from the pits of despair to a relief so great that it made her insides contract. She gripped his hand in both of hers, aware of James waiting somewhere behind her. She didn't want to talk to him right now. Maybe never. All her energy had to go toward Leo. Toward making sure he recovered.

Leo's eyes moved from hers to a spot just over her left shoulder. *"Papá, Papá ¿Dónde estás?"*

Mila's throat tightened to breaking point when she realized he wasn't asking where his dead father was but was looking at James.

She glanced back, pleading for him not to hurt Leo. Not now. His mouth moved, but nothing came out, the shock on his face so obvious it might have been funny under different circumstances. Only no one was laughing. Least of all her.

He gave her a long glance before coming forward, the smile he gave Leo as fake as a runway model's. And his posture. It was stiff. His muscles tensed and ready.

Ready to run. Again.

Well, good. She could only hope he did it before she told him to get the hell out of her life.

How dared he look her in the eye six years ago and tell her that he simply couldn't go through with their wedding when all the while he'd been sitting on the real reason.

And somehow his lie was so much worse than her aunt's had been. Because Mila had been an adult, fully capable of dealing with anything he'd handed to her. Only he hadn't given her the chance.

Well, she didn't care. This was about Leo. Not about her. Not about James. He could take his sorry little sack of confessions and saunter right back out of their lives. But not until he helped Leo get through this one last thing.

The child held out his hand and James took it. *"¿Estoy bien?"* Am I okay?

Mila's heart fragmented into a million pieces.

"Yes, Leo." There was a strangled edge to

James's voice that she didn't recognize. "You're going to be fine now. I promise."

She took a deep breath. At least this time he'd spoken the truth. She and Leo would be fine—without James. She would make sure of it, make sure she gave Leo everything he needed. And the thing he needed most was love.

The boy's eyelids fluttered, and Mila leaned down to kiss his brow. "You sleep. I'll be here when you wake up."

When she glanced back at James. There was an anguish in his expression that she recognized all too well. She'd seen it once before. In the church, right before their wedding.

Mila moved away from Leo, hoping James would follow her. She didn't want little ears to hear what she was about to say. She met him by the door.

"Thank you for finally telling me the truth after all these years, but I think you should go. Now, before he wakes up."

Even as she said the words, her heart cried out for him to say something—anything—that would change her mind before she could make the break complete, but he stood there like a stone.

She waited a second or two longer and when there was still nothing she finished the job, bringing down the ax before she lost her courage. "I want you to go, James. And don't come back."

Mila threw herself into her work like never before, flitting between her LA clinic and the new one. James had given her free rein over the hiring of staff, and Avery had helped her in selecting the best candidates and setting up shop.

James had left instructions that no expense should be spared. She had an open checkbook, and he wanted her to use it however she wanted.

Of course he hadn't told her that in person. He'd done as she'd asked. He'd left. In fact, she hadn't seen him in the last two weeks. Someone said he'd taken his sailboat and gone on an extended vacation.

Where?

It didn't matter.

What did matter was that her doubts about the way she'd ended things were beginning to crop up, multiplying like dust bunnies that crouched beneath her bed, hidden from view but there nonetheless.

He'd done what he'd thought best back then.

Had it been the right decision?

No. No more than her aunt had done the right thing by telling her that her parents had died in a car accident.

Had he done it with malicious intent?

No. Of that she had no doubt.

I was trying to protect you.

In truth, nothing could have protected her from the pain of him saying it was over. Or the pain of her parents' deaths. Both things had been devastating losses that she'd never gotten over.

But James had confessed on his own. She hadn't had to wave a newspaper article in his face.

Had she pushed him away too quickly, fearing that if she didn't he would just repeat the mistakes of the past and hurt her again? Well, she'd made sure he never had the chance of doing that.

But if he'd wanted to stay, wouldn't he have fought for her? Or come back later and tried to get her to change her mind? He hadn't done that six years ago, so why did she expect him to do it now?

Besides, she'd basically told him not to bother.

Scrubbing the exam table a little harder than

necessary after her last patient of the day, she tried to figure out what exactly she wanted.

She wanted James.

But did he really want her? Oh, he'd made love to her after that gala as if he cared about her. And he'd said that what he wanted to tell her had to do with the past...*and* the present. She'd never given him the chance to tell her anything beyond that awful confession.

But what else could he have wanted to say?

The door opened and Freya poked her head in. In her normal no-nonsense fashion she rounded the corner and braced her back against the wall beside the door, her maternity top skimming over her belly. Her friend glowed with health and happiness. And somehow that made Mila even more miserable. Especially since her cycle had come in with a vengeance, verifying what the pregnancy test had already told her. She wasn't carrying James's child. And if she was, would he have stayed with her just for that reason? He'd mentioned feeling a sense of responsibility toward that Cindy person when he'd thought she'd been pregnant.

More doubts arose, revealing the saddest truth of all.

She missed him. Terribly. Despite everything. As did Leo, who kept asking where Papá was.

That just about killed her.

She tossed her paper towel into the trash and tried to think of something cheery to say to her friend. She came up blank, settling for resting a hip against the exam table and waiting for Freya to spit out whatever it was she was chewing on.

"I know where he is."

A stab of something went through her system. "Where who is?"

Freya gave her a look.

"Okay. I know who you mean. He lied to me, Freya. About everything."

"I know. He told me." Her friend moved as close as she could without her belly touching Mila. "I tried waiting until one of you came to your senses, but since neither of you seems to be heading in that direction, I'm going to tell you something. And then you can decide what you want to do about it."

"Okay." Mila wasn't sure she wanted to hear

it, but if it would help her understand what had happened, maybe she could at least gain closure.

"James said he told you about Cindy. I had no idea. He never said a word. Until I confronted him on the phone a few days ago. Did he also tell you that our father had a habit of getting women pregnant and then paying them off to keep them quiet? Or that he offered to do the same with Cindy?"

"What?" James had said nothing about it. Not that she'd given him a chance.

"It's true. There are probably people walking around out there who have no idea that Michael Rothsberg is their father. Or that they have half-siblings." She paused. "James didn't say it outright, but I think that's why he broke off your engagement. So that he didn't become like our father, unwilling to face the consequences of his actions. If Cindy was pregnant, he wanted that child to know who its father was."

Mila gulped. It all made sense. Had she made a huge mistake?

"You're my friend, Freya. Couldn't you have asked him those questions back then?"

"When? After you'd left for Brazil and said you never wanted to hear James's name again?" Her shoulders twitched. "I was just as angry at him as you were, Mi. Then, after you came back to LA, I thought that bringing up the past would just hurt everyone involved."

She touched Mila's hand. "But now...I think he loves you, Mi. And this time, no matter how hurt you might feel, I don't think you should let him get off quite so easily."

Easily? None of this was easy. Would things have been any different if James had indeed told her the truth six years ago? She searched her heart.

No. Probably not. But now? Was she going to just let him drop a bombshell about their past and then walk away a second time?

Actually, he hadn't. She'd told him to leave. And he had. If he'd tried to express his undying love for her, she probably would have thrown it back in his face. She hadn't been ready to forgive him.

And now?

"What should I do?"

"Do you love him?"

Mila nodded.

"Can you live with what he did, knowing why he did it?"

Could she? She searched her heart. She hadn't

known about his dad. Or about Cindy. But James was a man of integrity, she'd seen that time and time again. He'd been trying to spare her in the best way he knew how.

"Yes. I think I can."

"Then if I were you, I'd hunt the man down and make him grovel. A lot. And then I'd forgive him."

Mila smiled. "I think I'm probably the one who needs to do the groveling. At least this time. I pushed him away, Freya, and didn't even give him a chance to finish explaining."

"Then maybe you should press Rewind and give him that chance."

"Maybe I should." She reached out and grabbed her friend up in a gentle hug. "But first you have to tell me where he is."

"I can do better than that. Zack knows this guy…"

By the time Freya had finished laying out the plan, Mila found something seeping into her heart that hadn't been there for the last six years: hope.

CHAPTER TWELVE

Someone was chasing him.

James had just pulled up anchor, not to mention pulling his head out of his ass and finally acknowledging what his heart had known all along. He couldn't live without her. He didn't know exactly how to make this right but he had to at least try.

He wanted it all. And that included Leo.

He'd hurt her twice. Once by leaving her at the altar, and once by sleeping with her before he'd told her the truth about what he'd done all those years ago. He wouldn't blame her if she told him to get the hell off her doorstep—well, technically it was *his* doorstep since she was staying in his guest house. That was if she hadn't already left.

Leo calling him Papá so soon after he'd told Mila the truth had been the last straw. He hadn't earned the right to be called that by anyone, least of all a young boy who'd known pain and fear most of his life. His reaction had been to run, instead of fighting for what he wanted.

But he was done running. Done allowing his life's course to be charted by his father's sins. And by his own past.

James was going to find Mila and tell her exactly what he'd wanted to tell her that day in Leo's hospital room. That he loved her. That he wanted to make this work, and he was willing to do whatever it took to make her forgive him for what he'd done.

He glanced back again. The dinghy was still there, bouncing over the choppy waters and zigzagging to avoid his wake.

What the hell? James was moving under his engine's power. He could just ramp up his speed or set his sails so that they would catch more of the wind and pull away from his pursuer with ease. It wasn't a coast-guard vessel. Maybe it was a member of the paparazzi, looking for more dirt on the Rothsberg family. As if there wasn't enough already.

And if the person decided to follow him farther offshore? They could get themselves into a situation that could turn deadly. He wasn't willing to risk it. It would be better to just cut speed and give the fool a piece of his mind.

Just then his phone pinged, signaling he'd received a text.

Perfect.

Suddenly, the normal stab of irritation was replaced by nerves. Or maybe a premonition.

Forgetting about the person behind him for a moment, he glanced at the screen of his cell phone.

Would you mind slowing down so I can catch you?

He blinked and looked closer. Mila's avatar was displayed at the top of the message.

Catch him?

He looked back again to see the person at the wheel was now waving at him like a crazy person.

Damn it!

Mila. What was she…?

He immediately cut the engine and turned the wheel so the bow would face into the wind. By the time the dinghy pulled alongside, he'd dropped anchor and had come over to the side to yell, "Throw me a line."

With hair plastered to her head and soaking wet

from head to toe from sea spray, she was still the most beautiful sight he'd ever seen. He'd been heading to LA to try to win her back. And she was here.

And she could have gotten herself killed!

She threw the rope, and James quickly lowered a couple of bumpers down the side of the sailboat to keep the vessels from slamming together in the current. He then tied the dinghy's line to one of the metal cleats on deck. Dropping the rope ladder he kept for swimming outings, he held it steady as Mila grasped the sides and began to climb. When she was close enough, he grabbed her hands and hauled her the rest of the way on board.

"Were you hoping to wind up like those Jet Skiers we ran into a few weeks back? What the hell were you thinking?"

"I was thinking I wasn't going to let the prince turn back into a toad for a second time."

He blinked at her. Maybe that ride out to him had been bumpier than he'd thought. "Come again?"

"Never mind." She took a step closer. "Freya told me what your father did to those women. What he tried to do to you."

Leave it to his sister to interfere. Although this time, maybe she'd been right to.

He swallowed hard. "That is one person I don't want to talk about ever again."

"You don't have to." She reached for his hand. "Let's talk about us instead."

A spark of something came to life in his chest. She'd said "us." As in there might be a chance for him to undo the mess he'd made? "You basically told me there was no us."

"I know. And I'm sorry. I should have heard you out."

"I was just heading back to make you do exactly that. And to ask you to forgive me."

"You were?" Her head tilted as if she was surprised.

"Yes."

She laughed. "Well, I guess I could have saved myself the trouble of hunting you down, then, couldn't I?" She glanced down at the dinghy.

"Is that thing even licensed?"

"Of course it is. And I caught you, didn't I?"

"You did. You look like you've driven one of those before." He had to admit she'd maneuvered the tiny boat beautifully.

"I have. Many times. In Brazil, while doing my medical missions." Her face turned serious as she gestured at his boat. "I do forgive you, but now that I'm here I have to tell you this scares me a little, James. It always has, even when we were together."

"What does?"

"The fancy boat, expensive fund-raisers, the world-class clinic." She glanced again at the dinghy bouncing far below them. "That little boat… is me. It's what I'm happy with. I believed for six years that I wasn't enough for you, and I'm afraid—"

"Not enough for me?" He grabbed her and hauled her to him. "You were always too much. Too beautiful. Too kind. Too…everything. And I didn't want what I'd done to somehow touch you and destroy everything you are. Just like my dad destroyed the lives of who knows how many women and children."

He kissed her cheek. "I never wanted kids, for that very reason. I'm scared too, Mi. Scared I won't be enough for Leo. For you."

"You are. Of course you are." She reached up and touched his face. "When I saw the way you looked at him…I knew I'd never stopped loving you."

He gulped, a wave of emotion sweeping up from his gut and moving to his lungs. His throat. His mouth. He tried to speak and failed, so he shook his head and then tried again. "You love me?"

"Yes." She wrapped her arms around his neck and pressed a tender kiss against his jaw. "Do you love me?"

"I always have." That one thing he did know. And right now, it was the only thing that was keeping him going.

"Then it's time we both stopped running from the truth and found a way to be together." She lifted her phone. "Text me back."

"What?"

"Freya says you haven't texted anyone in six years." She trailed light fingertips down the side of his temple. "So text me. Tell me you're going to stay with me this time—that you won't keep anything from me ever again. And…I'll believe you."

James tipped up her chin and slid his lips over hers. Once, twice, three times until he was in danger of dragging her down to his cabin and making love to her then and there. But that's not what she wanted. She'd asked him to do something, and he needed to do it. To make them both believe this could work.

Taking her hand, he went over to the steering console and picked up his phone. He slowly depressed the letters on the keypad, and then for several nerve-racking moments stared at the words he'd typed, his thumb hovering over the Send button. He pressed it. Set the cell phone back on the glossy teak surface beside him.

A tiny lion roared from somewhere nearby, ruining the seriousness of the moment. Mila's phone.

Smiling, her eyes on his, she drew the instrument out of her pocket and stared at the screen.

The words he'd typed were seared into his head, he could almost hear them spoken aloud as her eyes skipped across the text.

I love you, Mila. You and Leo. And anyone else who might be tucked inside you in the future. Will you marry me? We can do the whole damn wedding ceremony through texts, if you want—vows included. Just say you want to be with me.

Moisture rimmed her eyes, one tear sliding down her cheek. "I do. I want to be with you."

"Thank God." He brushed the tear from her face and then took the phone and laid it beside his own. "And now that we've gotten that out of the way, we won't be needing those for a while."

A smile came to her face. "No? And why is that?"

"Because I want any future communication to be up close and personal. Starting now."

With that, James swept her off her feet and headed below deck, where he wouldn't need texts to tell her how he felt. He planned to show her. From this moment and far into the future.

EPILOGUE

HE WAS STILL HERE.

The vows hadn't been texted, they'd been re-cited. Her wedding veil gently lifted. And he was kissing her. As if he couldn't get enough.

James hadn't run this time. And neither had she.

Clutching the lapels of his tuxedo, and sur-rounded by their friends from The Hollywood Hills Clinic and Bright Hope, Mila had all she could possibly need.

He finally let her up for air, and clapping erupted from all around them. Freya handed back her bou-quet, while Zack passed one of the pair's sleeping twins to his radiant wife. Now a year old, Tobey and Willow Carlton were a sight to behold this beautiful November day.

And Leo…

Mila's eyes sought him out and found him next to Rosa, the woman's arm protectively curled around his shoulders. He was out of his casts and walking with just the help of a crutch. Soon he wouldn't even need that. Adam Walker had performed a second surgery to do some fine-tuning of the tendons in his feet. It had gone wonderfully, and Adam, seated next to Gabriella and Rafael, two other doctors from James's clinic, said Leo would have normal function. An outcome Mila was extremely grateful for.

And soon Leo would be theirs. The adoption papers were due to be filed next week. His uncle had relinquished all rights and so the barriers were being lifted one by one.

Mila hadn't gotten pregnant during that infamous pool session, but she had a few months later. And this time the missing birth control had been intentional, James's way of physically proving to her that he would be there for her this time. She finally understood why she hadn't been able to make things work with Tyler. It was because she'd never stopped loving James. Thank God they'd both realized it in time.

Mila had also been right about Tyler and Avery. The couple had eloped two weeks ago. Her friend had sent her congratulations through Freya along with a promise to be back at work in a few days. She couldn't be happier.

Taking her hand and lifting it to his mouth, her new husband kissed the ring he'd just placed on her finger. "Don't ever take it off," he murmured.

"I won't."

And then they were running down the aisle of the church, past Flo and Nate, Lola and Jake, Grace and Liam, and so many others who had made their lives richer. The only one who wasn't there was Michael Rothsberg. Mila and James had agreed they weren't going to let him cast a pall over their lives a second time. But James's mom had come—and she'd offered to help Rosa with Leo until they got back from their honeymoon. She'd then kissed Mila's cheek and wished her many happy years. In turn, Mila had hugged her tight and thanked her for making James the man he was today.

"I can't take any credit for that, honey," she'd murmured in that mellow Southern drawl Mila had heard countless times in films. "James is the man he is because that's the man he decided to be."

And the man he'd decided to be was strong yet

compassionate. He'd avoided treating children for years, but for the first time he was considering teaming up with Mila for a medical mission. She'd go back to Brazil, where James would do reconstructive surgery on kids who so desperately needed it, while Mila did what she did best, provided health services to at-risk moms and children.

When they exited the church, she wasn't prepared for the flash of cameras everywhere as they ran toward the limousine. But, tucked against James's side, it was a small price to pay for the happiness she'd found.

One of her white high-heeled shoes caught in a crack on the sidewalk and popped off in midstride. It flipped end over end before landing on the pavement behind them. Soon it was lost in the sea of paparazzi that closed in on them.

"My shoe!" She hobbled forward a few feet, the difference of the lost inches on one foot slowing her down.

"Leave it." James scooped her up, her wedding dress billowing over his arm while the photographers seemed to eat it up. "Prince Charming might have needed a shoe to find his true love, but I don't. I have you right here. And I never intend to let you go."

With that, they climbed into the sleek black vehicle, and James proceeded to show her the truth of that statement. It was fine by Mila. Because she intended to do the same: to hang on to this man for the rest of her life.

* * * * *

We hope you enjoyed the final story in
THE HOLLYWOOD HILLS CLINIC *series*

*And, if you missed where it all started,
check out*

*SEDUCED BY THE HEART SURGEON
by Carol Marinelli*

*FALLING FOR THE SINGLE DAD
by Emily Forbes*

*TEMPTED BY HOLLYWOOD'S TOP DOC
by Louisa George*

*PERFECT RIVALS...
by Amy Ruttan*

*THE PRINCE AND THE MIDWIFE
by Robin Gianna*

*HIS PREGNANT SLEEPING BEAUTY
by Lynne Marshall*

*TAMING HOLLYWOOD'S ULTIMATE
PLAYBOY
by Amalie Berlin*

All available now!